DRUGSTORE IN ANOTHER WORLD
~ The Slow Life of a Cheat Pharmacist ~

NOVEL 3

WRITTEN BY
Kennoji

ILLUSTRATED BY
Matsuuni

Airship

Seven Seas Entertainment

CHEAT KUSUSHI NO SLOW LIFE:
ISEKAI NI TSUKURO DRUGSTORE VOL. 3

© HIFUMI SHOBO 2019
© Kennoji 2019
Originally published in Japan in 2019 by HIFUMI SHOBO Co., LTD.
English translation rights arranged through TOHAN CORPORATION, TOKYO.

No portion of this book may be reproduced or transmitted
in any form without written permission from the copyright
holders. This is a work of fiction. Names, characters, places,
and incidents are the products of the author's imagination
or are used fictitiously. Any resemblance to actual events,
locales, or persons, living or dead, is entirely coincidental.
Any information or opinions expressed by the creators of this
book belong to those individual creators and do not necessarily
reflect the views of Seven Seas Entertainment or its employees.

Seven Seas press and purchase enquiries can be sent to
Marketing Manager Lianne Sentar at press@gomanga.com.
Information regarding the distribution and purchase of
digital editions is available from Digital Manager CK Russell
at digital@gomanga.com.

Seven Seas and the Seven Seas logo are trademarks of
Seven Seas Entertainment. All rights reserved.

Follow Seven Seas Entertainment online at
sevenseasentertainment.com.

TRANSLATION: Elliot Ryouga
ADAPTATION: Kat Adler
LOGO DESIGN: George Panella
COVER DESIGN: Hanase Qi
INTERIOR LAYOUT & DESIGN: Clay Gardner
COPY EDITOR: Meg van Huygen
LIGHT NOVEL EDITOR: T. Anne
PREPRESS TECHNICIAN: Rhiannon Rasmussen-Silverstein
PRINT MANAGER: Lissa Pattillo
MANAGING EDITOR: Julie Davis
ASSOCIATE PUBLISHER: Adam Arnold
PUBLISHER: Jason DeAngelis

ISBN: 978-1-64827-448-0
Printed in Canada
First Printing: November 2021
10 9 8 7 6 5 4 3 2 1

MINA

REIJI

CONTENTS

1	Getting Silky Smooth	7
2	Soft and Warm	17
3	Cleaning Is War	27
4	A Cool Present	37
5	The Friendly, Totally-Not-Scary Neighborhood Goblin	47
6	Children Are Merciless	59
7	Chocolate Day	71
8	Colds Aren't Caught Out of Nowhere	83
9	Bathtime Panic	95
10	Toughening Up	105
11	Kirio Reiji's Studying Meds	117
12	Bad at Drinking Parties	127
13	That Seasonal Stuff	137
14	An Olive Branch	155
15	Sleep Versus Endless Rest	165
16	Smoopy-Doopy Skin	173
17	Herding Cats	181
18	A Real Ladies' Man	189
19	Stopping the Shocks	197
20	The Softness Contest	205
21	The Clean-Shaven King	215
	Afterword	225

1

Getting Silky Smooth

SINCE THE CHORES were done for the day, I was chilling out in the drugstore.

Once Mina noticed that Noela and Ejil were absent, she came over. "Mr. Reiji...um...I'd like to talk about something."

"Sure. What's up?" *Did she gain weight again?*

"I bet you just thought something incredibly rude," Mina scowled. "Do you think I'm going to tell you I've gained weight?!"

"Are you an esper or a detective or something?!" I groaned. *How did she guess that?!*

"Whatever. Since I *haven't* gained weight, it's fine." Mina almost sounded like she was bragging. "That said, you're right that this involves my appearance. Um..." She glanced around, then inched closer to my ear and whispered.

I was shocked. "You're seriously worried about *that*?"

"Yes! Anyone with a fair maiden's soul would be concerned! It's tough!"

Hunh. I never guessed that Mina thought about that kind of thing. "Do you think it bugs Noela too?"

"I wonder. She's kind of unique."

Yeah... I guess Noela's so fluffy, she might not pay attention to that.

Mina pressed her fingertips together. "U-up till now, whenever I've spotted any, I've taken care of them," she said in a hushed voice. "But..."

"I get it. That must be really annoying. You want something that gets rid of them all at once, right?"

Mina nodded.

"For a guy, I guess it might be a drag if the girl you liked didn't look after that," I reflected.

"Exactly," agreed Mina. "I don't think that's unique to men either. Women prefer guys to look after those things. Your shins have bothered me lately, to be honest."

"My shins?" I echoed. "Uh, but it's kind of a different story for dudes, right?"

Still, it would've been easy to get superficial. I figured lots of women would be happy with that. *I bet there're other girls like Mina out there.*

"Hey!" Paula came in, waving. "I see you're free as always, Rei Rei!"

GETTING SILKY SMOOTH

"You're the last person I want to hear *that* from," I retorted.

Mina bowed her head politely. "Good day, Paula."

"Hey, Paula, do you do that too?" I blurted out.

Paula was obviously confused. "Uh...what're the deets?"

Mina quietly explained.

"Oh. Well...yeah, sure," Paula replied. "I *am* a young woman dating around, you know. To be honest, I think most people do that. You do too, right, Anna?"

Paula turned, revealing that Annabelle had been in the drugstore for a while.

They must've met up on the way here. Wait...Paula calls her "Anna"?

"Er...yeah, I guess." Annabelle looked away, embarrassed.

"Really, Captain?" I asked. "That's surprising."

"Well, gee whiz, sorry." Annabelle glanced at me awkwardly. "Anyhow, uh...this isn't the kind of conversation to hold at the pharmacy."

I get it. This kind of thing's normally "girl talk."

"You see," Mina explained to our two visitors, "I just asked Mr. Reiji to formulate something that makes the process nice and quick."

"Oh, I get it!" Paula and Annabelle replied in tandem.

"If customers want something like that, I could whip it up and put it on sale," I mused.

"Please do!"

Damn, that didn't take much. They really want it badly, huh?

I left the three women behind and headed to the lab.

When I thought about it, lots of female customers came to the drugstore for beauty products. It wasn't an understatement to say that tons of women wanted to stay beautiful as long as possible.

As I finished my work, Noela popped her head in. "Master, Noela bored."

"Then go help Mina. I think she still has housework."

"Leave to me! What that, Master?" Noela pointed at the new concoction.

I laughed like a mad scientist. "It's a treatment to make women beautiful! If you used it the wrong way, though, it'd be real bad news."

> **HAIR-REMOVAL CREAM:** Contains hair-dissolving particles. Suppresses hair growth.

From the way the three women described their hair-removal troubles, it hadn't sounded as though they were unique cases. I was betting that the cream would be a big hit with female customers. Once I'd made several bottles,

GETTING SILKY SMOOTH

I took three back to the store and guided the girls to the washroom.

"This stuff here will take care of hair really fast. It's just what you wanted." I showed them the bottles. "It's called hair-removal cream."

They gulped loudly, focusing on the new product. "Hair-removal cream?"

It'd be fastest just to show them. I spread a tiny bit of the cream on my arm. "Let it sit for five minutes, then gently wash it off. After that..."

"After that...?" The trio directed their serious gazes at my forearm.

I rubbed off the water, revealing a hairless, silky-smooth patch of skin to everyone present. The girls gasped in shock, then applauded.

"Wow, that's amazing, Mr. Reiji!" exclaimed Mina. "Thank you so much! Now I won't need to spend all that time in the bath, battling my hair!"

"You're a super-duper legit genius, Rei Rei!" agreed Paula. "That stuff's really crazy. It takes, like, no effort!"

Even Annabelle nodded, satisfied with the hair-removal cream's results.

To be extra sure, I had the girls test the cream themselves on the backs of their hands. It seemed to go fine.

"So, you worry about excess hair too, Annabelle?" Mina asked.

"Oh, shut up. Is that so bad?" Annabelle huffed.

"Of course not!" Mina replied. "It just makes me think you're a girl like us, that's all."

Turning bright red, Annabelle tossed her wallet directly at my face.

"Ow."

"T-take as much as you want, you big jerk!" Grabbing a single bottle of hair-removal cream, she rushed out of the drugstore, still beet-red.

What the heck's her deal?

I didn't know how much money was in Annabelle's wallet, but I hadn't intended to charge her, since she tested the new product for me. *I'll give back the wallet tomorrow morning, when she drops by for her potions.*

"Anna's a real cutie," Paula whispered, staring at the spot where the captain had been.

"Yeah," Mina replied. "This time, I actually agree."

I told Paula that she didn't need to pay me; after that, she and Mina locked me out of the washroom. I figured they wanted to use the hair-removal cream right away. I was interested in what was going on, but I would've had my ass handed to me if I'd peeked, so I slipped away.

GETTING SILKY SMOOTH

In the lab, I grabbed the remaining bottles of the hair-removal cream prototype and headed back to the storefront.

Wait. There's a bottle missing. Did I miscount?

Before long, Mina and Paula came out of the washroom.

"Look, Mr. Reiji!" Mina exclaimed. "I'm all smooth now!"

"What's your ulterior motive for getting me this silky-smooth, Rei Rei?" cackled Paula.

The two looked thrilled with the hair-removal cream's results. Unfortunately, I had no way of knowing what had gone on behind the scenes.

◆◆◆

The next day, I got up at the usual time, doing my best to ignore the racket elsewhere in the house.

"Good morning, Mr. Reiji," Mina smiled.

"Morning." I sat down in the dining room. As Mina cooked breakfast, I asked casually, "Did that cream cause any weird side effects?"

"Nope! Not a thing." Mina glanced at Noela. "Um… not for me, at least."

Noela was sitting next to me, and she didn't look any

different than usual. *Well, except for the scarf around her tail. Why would she bundle her tail up? She's usually so proud of it. Did she use the cream?*

I turned to Noela. "Aren't you dressed up today? Did something happen?"

"Garoo?! I-It nothing!"

Burning with curiosity, I pulled up the scarf to peek.

"Master! No touch! Pervert!" Noela quickly put some distance between us.

Too late for that. I'd already seen what I needed to. The scarf wasn't a fashion statement; Noela's prized fur was gone. She'd snuck out a bottle of hair-removal cream when I wasn't looking. "You used the cream, didn't you?"

"I told you he'd find out, Noela," Mina interjected. "This is what happens when you try whatever Mr. Reiji makes without listening to the instructions carefully."

Noela's ears drooped sadly. "Arroo..."

According to Mina, Noela had noticed what happened this morning. The cream was supposed to be beautifying, yet her tail's fluffy fur was gone! She'd been afraid that she would get in trouble if I found out she used the cream, so she'd gone to Mina about it.

"That explains why the house was so loud this morning," I mused.

"N-no worry," Noela stammered. "Grow back soon."

GETTING SILKY SMOOTH

"Hmm. I don't know about that, Noela," I replied. "That cream also suppresses hair growth."

"Arroo?!"

Pitter patter! Noela trotted close and tugged at my cuff. "Sorry! Sorry! Noela no use without asking anymore!"

"All right, all right! Just stop pulling my sleeve!"

Noela clung to me tearfully. I patted her head, since no other choice was available to me. After she let go, I grabbed the hair-growth shampoo I'd formulated for Zeral.

"If you use this, your tail fur should come back," I told Noela. "The hair-removal cream doesn't stop growth completely."

"Thank you, Master!" Noela sniffled, wiping her tears away. "Noela stay by Master's side forever."

I didn't get mad at her. At the end of the day, Noela was just a young girl. Girls her age were usually interested in beauty, since it attracted guys. In fact, everyone—male and female—had that instinct.

The next day, Noela's fluffy tail was back to normal. She never tested new products without asking again.

16

DRUGSTORE in Another World
~ The Slow Life of a Cheat Pharmacist ~

Soft and Warm

"ACHOOOO!" I sneezed. *That was loud enough to scare even me!*

It'd been chilly lately, and the sun set way earlier. Judging by the temperature, we were closer to winter than fall.

As I kept watching the store, Noela trotted over. "Okay, Master?"

"Yeah, I'm fine. Thanks." Noela didn't seem even slightly cold, probably because she was so fluffy. "How about you? Are you cold?"

"Warmer than most human."

I knew it. All that fur keeps her toasty. I patted my lap. She happily plopped down on it. "What's up, Master?"

Poof! I gave all of Noela—including her swinging tail—a bear hug. *Holy crap. She's crazy warm! What the heck?!*

Noela's perfect temperature was probably due to a combination of things. Her fur seemed to hold heat, and not only was it fluffy, but it was nice and smooth too. I sat there for a while, hugging Noela like a huge stuffed animal.

With her, I can make it through winter easily. I can even stay nice and warm at night if I stuff her in my bed.

"I'm back!" Returning home from shopping, Mina gave me a puzzled look. "Huh? Why're you clinging to Noela like that, Mr. Reiji?"

"For the record, there's nothing weird going on here," I promised Mina.

"Of course not. If there were, I'd be furious."

"Noela's just super warm. I'm stealing her body heat."

"Stealing Noela's heat?!" The furry ears below my chin twitched a few times. I squeezed them in both hands, finding them quite warm as well.

"Now, Mr. Reiji, you're scaring her. If you're too cold, should I fetch you a jacket?"

"No need with Noela here."

The werewolf girl looked at me. "Noela being useful to Master?"

"Yes, you are!"

"Garroo!" She wagged her tail.

She's so soft and warm. Hugging her feels amazingly comfy. In my position, Ejil would probably be beside himself.

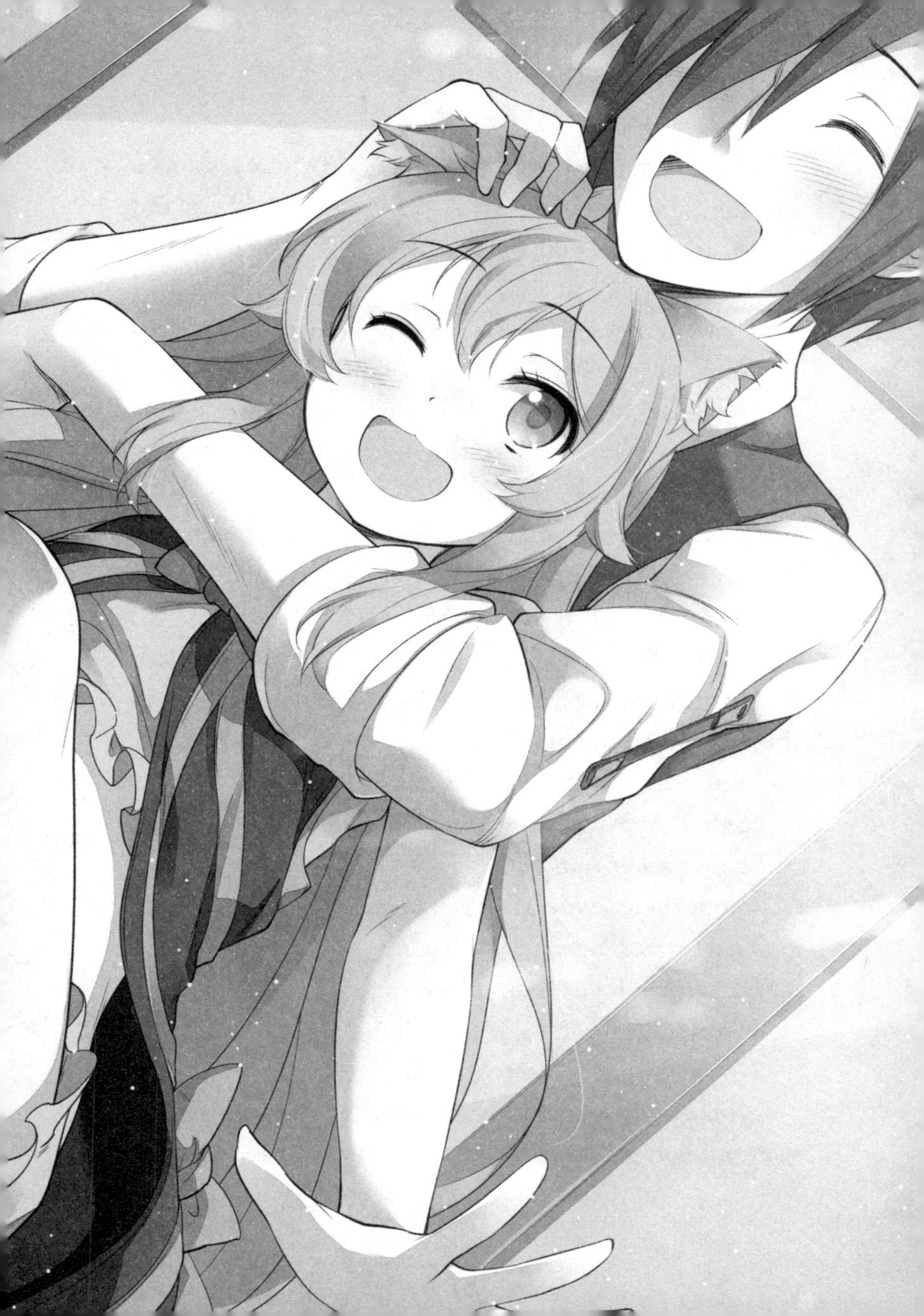

"Noela certainly is warm." Mina nodded. "We share a bed now and then."

"Wanna try sleeping in *my* bed, Noela?" I offered.

"'Kay."

"That's improper! Noela's a young woman, after all."

"Noela sleep in Master's bed! Useful!"

"Noela says it's all right," I pointed out to Mina.

"Absolutely not!" Mina frowned, refusing to listen further.

I doubt I'll get a full night's super-fluffy, super-warm sleep as long as Mina lives. Oh, right, she's dead. "What about you, Mina? Aren't you cold?"

"Hmm... Well, I'd be lying if I said no," Mina confessed. "My fingers and toes are especially chilly." Putting down the stuff she'd bought, she touched my cheeks.

"Whoa! You're freezing!"

"Right?" She giggled.

She seems happy about it.

"Come here, Noela! My hands are *frigid*!" Mina reached toward Noela.

The werewolf girl frantically dodged. "No cold!"

"If you stay on Mr. Reiji's lap, I'll catch you!"

"Noela's throne! Give to no one!"

Mina gently squeezed Noela's cheeks, tittering as the werewolf girl panicked.

SOFT AND WARM

"Hey, don't forget you're sitting on my knees!"

They're like sisters, I thought. *Hmm...I guess Mina's sensitive to the cold. Lots of women are. It might not be an understatement to say that Mina needs Noela more than I do.*

"But there's only one Noela," I mumbled.

How did I manage winter back in my other world? Stoves...kotatsu... Oh, right! "Guess I know what I need to make!"

Noela had long since vacated my knees; she was facing off with Mina. Hearing my announcement, they stopped and turned to me.

"What're you making, Mr. Reiji?"

"It's a surprise." I stood up.

Mina collected herself. "Then I'll prepare dinner while I wait to be surprised."

Noela followed me and Mina back into the house. "Noela help Master!"

"You're on store duty."

"No customers."

"Don't say that!"

I chased Noela back to the drugstore. It was already dark out, so I doubted anyone would swing by, but an employee who wasn't busy needed to watch the shop.

In the lab, I followed my medicine-making skill's

directions, gathering ingredients. Fortunately, I had a decent stockpile of medicinal herbs, so I didn't need to go outside. When I finished mixing the bottled liquid, it glowed as always.

> **INSTA-WARM**: Generates heat (about 40 degrees Celsius) for several hours when shaken.

"Awesome. It's done."

I divided the fluid between a small bottle for day-to-day use and a large bottle for bedtime. I gave the small bottle a few shakes, testing it—sure enough, it warmed up. It wasn't scorching or lukewarm.

"This is the perfect temperature," I murmured.

Bottle in hand, I headed to the kitchen, where Mina was doing dishes. *Oh, right. In this world, there's no hot water for dishwashing.*

"It's ready, Mina. This's the stuff." I showed her the vial.

She looked at it and blinked, clearly mystified. "That was certainly fast! What exactly is it?" Wiping her hands on her apron, she took the bottle. "Oh, you used warm water?"

I chuckled and answered her question with a question. "How does someone boil water, Mina?"

"Um, by lighting a fire and—"

SOFT AND WARM

"Well, this bottle's full of special water that gets warm without a fire."

I poured another vial of insta-warm, telling Mina to shake it.

She shook it hard. "Just doing this will warm the water? I'm not heating it or anything."

"Patience, young lady."

"Are you playing a trick, Mr. Reiji? Wait...w-wow!" As if a chick were hatching in her hands, Mina began to freak out. She kept looking at the vial. "Oh my gosh! Mr. Reiji, this is incredible! It's so warm!"

"Right?" I gave her my most victorious smirk of the day. "It'll stay hot for hours, so feel free to pocket it. When your fingers get too cold, just touch the bottle."

Mina gulped with a deadly serious expression. "I'll always be warm."

"Bingo. I also have a bigger bottle for the bed. You can use that tonight."

"Gosh, thank you so much, Mr. Reiji!" Mina clasped my hand firmly. "You're my fingertips' savior!"

"Talk about a niche savior."

"I'm sure women will love this. Most have cold fingers during winter. I'm a run-of-the-mill girl, so I know what I'm talking about!"

She must really be happy with the insta-warm. Trusting

the self-proclaimed "run-of-the-mill girl," I headed to the lab to make more of the new product. I'd put it on the shelves tomorrow.

Eventually, Mina called me to dinner. I closed the store and sat at the dining table with Noela.

"New stuff done?" she asked.

"Yup. Check it out." I handed Noela a vial of insta-warm. "Hot, right? Now, we have nothing to fear from the cold." Her expression showed her concerned. *Weird.*

"That insta-warm's really amazing, Noela," Mina added. "I won't have to drag you to bed with me anymore."

"Arroo! Warm...is problem," Noela whispered to herself.

How so?

♦◆♦

To answer that question, I had to wait for the next morning. I'd tested a bottle of insta-warm overnight, and it was damn nice; under my blankets, it felt like spring had come.

This product's gonna sell like crazy, I thought, still drowsy. *It's warm, but soft. Even kinda fluffy.*

"Time to get up, Mr. Reiji!" called Mina, coming in. "I know your bed's cozy, but you have to get to work. Hmm? Something's odd about your blanket..."

SOFT AND WARM

Fwoosh! Mina tore away the blanket, revealing the fluffy "insta-warm."

"What's the big idea?" I whined. "It's cold."

"Ah! I wondered where Noela went!"

Why's Mina being so loud? I opened my eyes, only to see a large, white tail—not unlike a fluffy cat toy—in front of me.

"Awake, Master!" Noela was curled up next to me. Her ears twitched happily.

"Huh? What're you doing in here?"

It's cold! I shivered, searching for the insta-warm I'd put under the blanket. Strangely, it was nowhere to be found. *What the...? Where'd it go?*

Mina turned toward Noela. "So you were in Mr. Reiji's bed? No wonder I couldn't find you!"

I reached out to take back my blanket, but Mina dodged me swiftly.

With no other choice, I sat up and yawned widely, crossing my legs. "So, uh, why's Noela in my bed? And where'd my insta-warm go?"

Seriously. I knew for a fact that I'd slipped it into the bed. My toes were nice and warm until I fell asleep.

"Noela threw away."

"Why?"

"Making Master warm is Noela's job." She rolled toward me and slipped into my lap.

Yeah, she's definitely warm.

"I see. So, that's what happened," said Mina.

"Pardon me?"

"Noela was unhappy about your new insta-warm stealing her role as your heater."

"So she tossed it?" I looked at Noela inquisitively.

"Secret," the werewolf replied.

How could I get mad at this girl? I decided to stop using the insta-warm, since it made Noela jealous. "It's not cold under my blankets," I assured her, stroking her head.

She nodded. I doubted she'd climb into my bed anymore.

As we'd expected, the insta-warm became a customer favorite, thanks to its warmth, portability, and ability to keep folks cozy overnight. It was popular with male customers, but as Mina predicted, it was a huge hit with women—it became a number one seller.

Cleaning Is War

MINA AND NOELA had gone shopping this morning. After seeing them off, Ejil and I relaxed, watching the store. It was super cold, and our breath was white as snow, even inside the drugstore.

"During winter, I usually have my minions clean the castle top to bottom," the demon king told me.

"Seriously?"

"Of course. How could we conquer anyone without a clean, organized castle?"

"I'm honestly not sure I'd *want* the demon king's castle squeaky clean." I would've preferred chambers full of dusty floors, mold, spiderwebs, and so on. Keeping it clean weakened his "evil" image.

"Anyway, my underlings are terrible at housework," Ejil continued. "It's extremely irritating."

"Then why don't you do it? I'm sure you've got cleaning magic. Stop blaming them for everything."

"A-all right." Ejil took a notebook out of his bag and jotted, *"Stop blaming underlings for everything. Set a good example as the boss by doing things yourself."*

Hunh, I mused. *My resident demon king's taking this very seriously.*

As Ejil closed the notebook, I noticed the title on the cover: *Dr. Reiji Quotes.*

"Stop transcribing those!" I exclaimed. "It's embarrassing!"

"Why?! I've made a point of recording anything you say that touches my heart," Ejil retorted. "They're precious teachings you passed down to your student!"

"I never signed off on that, and I'm not your teacher! Precious teachings? Who am I, Confucius?"

I tried to snatch the notebook, but Ejil *was* the demon king. Needless to say, he dodged my attacks effortlessly. Three minutes later, I was exhausted; I gave up.

"About that cleaning magic you mentioned," Ejil said. "I don't possess anything like that. Do humans have that kind of ability?"

"Don't ask me. I'm a pharmacist, not a mage."

"Could you make some?"

"Pardon?"

"Some cleaning magic?"

"Like hell! What've you seen going on during your time at the drugstore?!" I'd only formulated medication and related drugstore products—never once had I created "magic."

"What do you mean?" Ejil gawked at me as though I were crazy. "I've seen you make the impossible possible!"

"You make me sound like some snake oil salesman," I objected. "The type running a crazy religious cult." *Still, I guess I understand why he sees me that way. I do make medicine that helps people with problems.*

"Ah! I see what you're getting at." Ejil sighed. "Up until now, you've prescribed me countless treatments, yet I've never properly thanked you."

"No, that's not the issue. I'm not refusing to create magic because you haven't acted appreciative or anything." *I literally can't make magic.*

"If you create magic that cleans the castle nice and fast, I'll be sure to prepare a proper reward for you this time," Ejil promised. "I'll use teleportation magic to deliver a selection of my army's sexiest succubi."

I guess he really put some thought into making me happy. "Please don't."

"That wouldn't be to your liking?"

"Look, that's not the issue. I don't need a reward."

"Doctor..." Ejil shot me a passionate gaze.

"Seriously, it's impossible for me to make cleaning magic," I began. "Wait... My medicine-making skill's reacting. I uh, guess I might be able to help."

"Doctor!" Ejil leapt toward me.

I grabbed his face to keep him at a distance. "I'm going to go whip something up. You watch the store."

"Yes, Doctor!"

I locked myself away in my lab, mixing the drugstore's men's body wash with our dish soap and strengthening their cleansing ingredients. My medicine-making skill wasn't telling me that I could make magic—I was still creating some kind of drugstore product.

EXTRA-STRENGTH ULTRA CLEANING GEL: Universal detergent. Wipes any surface sparkling clean.

Immediately, I put some gel on a rag to test my new creation. The lab had gotten kind of grimy, so I lightly wiped the floor.

Sparkle! The spot ended up remarkably clean—almost shiny.

"Wh-whoa! This is crazy!"

I ended up tidying the lab and wiping down the whole floor. The cleaning gel immediately revealed the true,

CLEANING IS WAR

natural color of every spot the rag passed over. *What the hell?! This is a blast!*

"Doctor, what's wrong?" Ejil popped in to check on me. He'd apparently heard my surprised cry.

"Look at this!"

"Holy—the lab looks brand-new!"

Right?!

"It was all cluttered and dirty!" Ejil continued. "I'd given up on scrubbing the spills everywhere! But now..."

The demon king really did love cleanliness. "Hey, how about we make the drugstore and house sparkle before Mina and Noela get home?"

"Heh heh! Sounds good. Let's do this."

"First, the living room!"

"Woo-hoo!"

Rags and cleaning gel in hand, Ejil and I waged war on the room.

"I'll handle the walls!" I exclaimed.

"Leave the floor to me!"

"Everyone knows you clean from top to bottom, dummy! Aren't you a king?! Follow tradition!"

"Yes, Doctor! 'Kings must follow tradition.' Got it!"

"Stop taking notes! Clean the windows."

"Roger that!"

"Loosen your shoulders, Ejil! Didn't I tell you to scrub with your left hand?! Treat your rag gently!"

"Apologies, sir!"

"Don't you want to see Noela's thrilled face?"

"Yes, Doctor! Wait—I get it now! If I tell her my feelings just as she sees the squeaky-clean living room, she'll surely respond in kind!"

"No way."

"Aw…all right."

"Anyhow, repeat after me—my rag is my brother-in-arms!"

"My rag is my brother-in-arms!"

The two of us got a bit carried away; we conquered the living room with ample energy left over. That momentum carried us through cleaning the dining room, the kitchen, my bedroom, the bathrooms, and even the storefront.

All right! The last stop is Mina and Noela's room! It wasn't like they'd ever forbidden me to enter. Still, I found myself weirdly nervous as we began cleaning.

Ejil seemed to be in the same boat. Tidying almost robotically, he pointed at a dresser. "Doctor, should I wipe that down?"

"I wouldn't if I were you, Ejil. Do you want Mina and Noela to kill you too?"

CLEANING IS WAR

I'd once approached that dresser by accident, and the girls raked me over the coals for it. It hadn't taken me long to realize what was in the drawers.

"Th-that dresser's even dangerous to you, Doctor? In that case, I should really..." Ejil whispered gravely to himself.

After he and I finished cleaning, I heard Mina and Noela's voices in the drugstore.

"Huh? Oh, gosh! The store's so clean!"

"Sparkling!"

They must've gotten back from shopping. I headed into the store; as I'd planned, the women were looking around, stunned. "It's not just the store. You should check out the rest of the house."

Mina let out a gasp. "Why didn't you say something, Mr. Reiji? I know you're busy with work. I would've gladly cleaned!"

"It's totally fine. I wanted to surprise you both."

She whacked me gently. "Gosh, you're wonderful. I'll make your favorite for dinner tonight!"

Noela, meanwhile, inspected every last corner. Impressed, she raised her voice. "Master work hard. Amazing!" Leaping onto me, she patted my head gently.

"By the way, where's Ejil?" Mina asked. "I don't see him anywhere."

"Oh, he's probably still in your room. He was cleaning too."

"H-huh? In our room?"

"Don't worry, we just cleaned—nothing else."

The three of us went to see how Ejil was faring.

"Yo, Ejil!" I called. "You done cleaning?"

There was no response.

Is he not in there? I opened the bedroom door, revealing the sparkling-clean walls and floor. Ejil, however, had collapsed in a pool of his own nose blood in front of the girls' dresser. He was clutching a pair of Mina's underwear. Mina and Noela stared at the demon king as though he were a pile of stinky trash.

I'd figured that they kept their underwear in those drawers; I'd cautioned Ejil that even *I* got in trouble for approaching that sacred black box. Unfortunately, he'd lost to the double whammy of curiosity and lecherousness. *He must've passed out before accomplishing his main goal,* I mused.

As I expected, the two girls nailed the unconscious Ejil with harsh kicks that hurled him through the window. *I'm pretty sure I heard something crack. Oh, well.*

"I figured that'd happen," I muttered, heading outside to bring the victim a potion. Ejil lay on the side of the road like an abandoned rag; I lifted him in my arms.

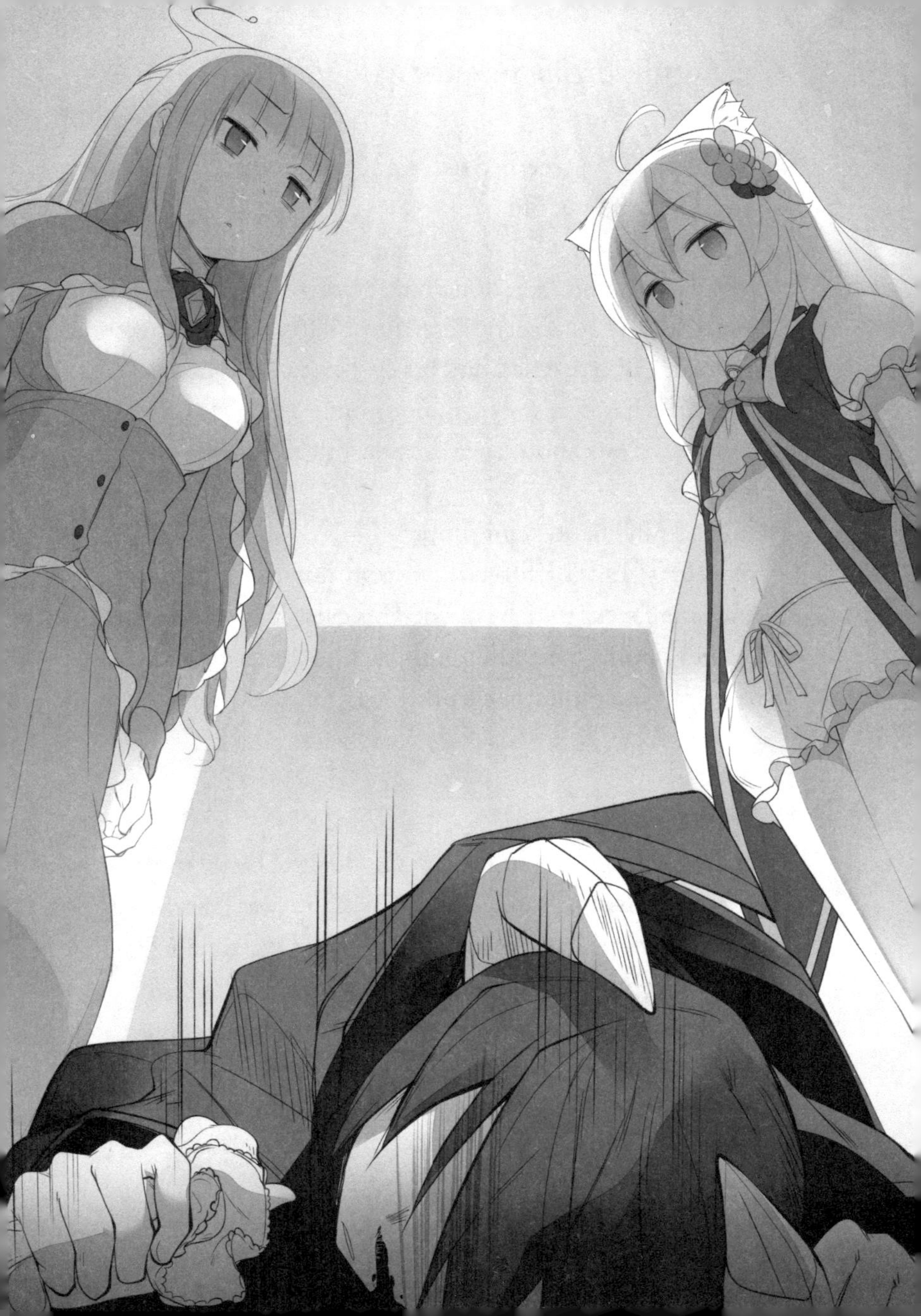

"D-Doctor..." Ejil seemed to have a hard time breathing.

"You lost this one, Ejil."

"I...I couldn't do it."

"It's all right, bud. You don't have to say anything else."

"How...did they react? Were they...happy about the clean house?" Ejil reached out, his eyes empty and lifeless.

I took his hand in my own, nodding. "The girls were, uh, pretty furious about that dresser. But not about the cleaning."

"I...see." Ejil's hand went limp.

"Ejil? Hey, Ejil!" I forced a potion down his throat, slapping his cheeks until he opened his eyes. *Yup, still alive.*

I made a point of sending him back to his castle with some extra-strength ultra cleaning gel.

◆◆◆

Later, Ejil swung by to inform me that the castle took a paltry two days to clean. Needless to say, he was grateful.

"I can't live without this cleaning gel!" he exclaimed. It was clear just how useful the product was to him.

The demon king's favorite extra-strength ultra cleaning gel became one of the drugstore's best-selling products, proving useful to households throughout Kalta.

4

A Cool Present

IT WAS OUR FIRST TIME eating at the Rabbit Tavern in a while, and Rena brought us a dish we definitely hadn't ordered.

"Thank you so much for those fish the other day, Mr. Pharmacist." The barmaid smiled. "This is our way of showing our gratitude."

"Aww. You didn't have to—"

Before I finished my sentence, Noela reached for the plate of steamed shellfish and helped herself. *Her appetite has no brakes.* Beside her, Mina dined daintily. Earlier, she'd told Noela to make sure to chew properly, like a grandmother would've.

"How were the fish, anyway?" I asked Rena. "Were diners pleased?"

"Totally! And we dried and smoked the leftovers so we could hold on to them longer."

Makes sense. This world doesn't have fridges or freezers, so people do that to keep food from spoiling.

"What about holding on to vegetables?" I asked. "They rot so fast, and they cost an arm and a leg. It must be tough."

"It really is!" Mina chimed in.

Meanwhile, Noela used a shell to scoop up the broth on the plate. *Mind your manners, Noela.*

"Speaking of," I added, "Mina, you only make salad on the day you buy veggies, right?" She typically cooked the vegetables she served on other days.

"Oh, you noticed? That's right! Noela doesn't seem to mind eating old vegetables, but as the one in charge of cooking, I'd hate to upset anyone's stomach."

"Always cooking vegetables sounds like a hassle."

"It is!"

I looked at my pasta. *Man, now that I think about it, I haven't had sashimi since I arrived here.* This world's oceans and rivers were far from Kalta, and preserving fish was impossible. Plus, I didn't think this town had that kind of cuisine—you know, raw fish and all. *Maybe I should try to build a fridge.*

Mina seemed to be having a blast talking about

homemaking. Standing up, I passed her my wallet. "Here. Pay with this."

"Where're you heading? Today's our day off."

"Yeah, I know. I've just got some stuff to do."

Noela licked her plate with all her might; there must've been lots of shellfish broth left. *Mind your manners, Noela... Eh, she's fine.*

Leaving the Rabbit Tavern, I headed to Paula's tool shop. She was probably watching the store, since she knew Kirio Drugs was closed today.

"Hello!" I called, entering. I found Paula slouched over the counter, asleep. "Hey, you've got a customer. Wake up!"

Paula's shoulders moved. She raised her head, her glasses totally askew. "Huh? Wha...? A customer? Liar."

"It's me, you goof."

"I ain't lending you money."

"I'm not a swindler!" *I swear, she can be such a dummy.* She didn't think of "Kirio Reiji" as anyone more than the owner of the store where she killed time, so she didn't recognize my voice.

Paula rubbed her eyes, adjusting her glasses. "Er, welcome, I guess."

"There we go. I knew you could do it."

She grinned, her chin firmly in her hands. "So what's the big idea? Wait—I know."

No, she definitely doesn't know.

"You got lonely because your big sis didn't vis—"

"Nope."

"Did you really have to cut me off like that?" Paula frowned.

"Hey, could you make me a big iron box?" I asked, picturing a refrigerator. I told Paula I could live with a small, one-door design if necessary, although that wouldn't be as big as a family fridge.

"If I hit up a craftsman, that should be doable," Paula replied. "But why do you need that?"

"I'm starting a food revolution in our little town."

"Whoa. Well, doesn't that sound fun? I want in."

I hadn't given her any details, but she was already on board, as I'd expected. "Listen up, Paula. Here're the deets." We discussed the specifics of the fridge, and I wrote them down.

"There are definitely parts I'll have to consult a craftsman about, but this should be doable," Paula confirmed.

"Excellent."

"If it actually works, it really *will* be a revolution. Amazing!"

"I'm counting on you!"

We exchanged a firm handshake, and I left the tool

A COOL PRESENT

shop. I had business to take care of—specifically, mass-producing icy gel and creating a new product.

My first objective was to make a simple refrigerator prototype. Paula had said it would take a craftsman about two days to finish the iron box. I was a bit worried about how quick that seemed, but Paula had been confident.

"I'm gonna tell 'em to prioritize my order," she'd said. "Just leave it to your favorite Paula!"

I got to work in the lab. "Okay, this should do the trick!"

> **PRESERVATIVE:** Prevents rot when exposed to air.

The stuff inside the bottle was liquid; it was the type of preservative you let sit uncovered.

Noela and Mina finally got home. They gave me puzzled looks as I worked in the lab.

"Today's your day off, Mr. Reiji," Mina reiterated. "Shouldn't you stop working so much?"

"Thanks, but I've just got a little to finish."

"All right, I understand. In that case, good luck!" She closed the lab door, smiling.

When I finish, she'll be blown away.

♦♦♦

Two days later, the iron box arrived at Paula's tool shop. I headed over with two different liquids. The box was in the center of the store, and it was small enough to wrap your arms around. Paula sat atop it.

"It's just like you asked for, right, Rei Rei?"

The box was about knee height, and its depth seemed perfect. The durable iron plating was as thin as possible.

"Oh, man." I smiled. "This really might get cold enough."

Paula and I immediately coated the interior with icy gel. A while later, I grabbed the box's wooden handle and opened the door; cold air blasted my face.

Paula stuck her arms inside the box. "Whoa! This is awesome! It's friggin' ice-cold!"

"Bah, come on. You're exaggerating." *Still, I get how she feels.* I couldn't have told you the box's exact temperature, but it definitely felt wintry.

"There's no point if this doesn't *stay* super cold, though," Paula added.

"I know." That was why I'd made so much icy gel. *If I spread a bunch over the interior, it'll stay cold for—*

"I'm climbing in for a sec!"

"Er, excuse me? What do you—wait, you're already inside?!"

Before I wrapped my head around her proclamation, Paula shut the makeshift fridge's door, closing herself in.

A COOL PRESENT

Ten minutes went by, and she didn't say a word. *Are you okay, Paula?* I opened the fridge. Paula fell out like a frozen statue, her face completely blue.

"Ish...super...cold..." she said through chattering teeth.

Oh, right. I forgot that icy gel almost works too *well.* I wrapped a warm blanket around Paula and headed back to the drugstore to take care of some work.

That evening, I swung by the tool shop to check on the fridge. *Yup, still cold. This should work perfectly as a refrigerator.*

I plopped the super-duper ice-cold fridge on a shopping cart and dragged it home, where Mina was doing dishes.

"Yo, do you have a sec?" I called.

"Of course. I didn't notice you come in. Where'd you get off to?"

"I was just at Paula's for a bit." That wasn't important, though. I brought Mina over to the fridge.

"What is this, Mr. Reiji?"

"Erm, it's called a refrigerator. It's a mysterious box that's super cold inside."

"Hunh." Mina didn't seem to understand.

Well, that's not her fault. It didn't exist here until earlier today. "Basically," I explained, "when you put fish, meat, veggies, and stuff inside it, it'll keep them cold for as long as you want."

"Really? All those different foods?"

"Yeah. Which means...?"

"They'll take longer to spoil?"

"Bingo!"

"What?!" Mina cried. She opened the fridge door. Stunned, she shrieked, "That's incredible!"

"This is yours, Mina. Consider it a present from me."

"A-are you sure? Th-this thing's truly astonishing, you know!"

"No worries. I'll make another one if a request comes in. I want to make sure this one works right anyway." I grinned.

Mina was overflowing with enthusiasm. "I'm going to make you all kinds of delicious dishes, Mr. Reiji!"

"I'm looking forward to it."

"You better be!" Her smile was as bright as a freshly bloomed sunflower.

I get it now. I probably did this because I wanted to make Mina happy. In a way, it's a present to myself.

At least, that was what crossed my mind at the time.

◆◆◆

A few days later, I learned that Paula had followed me home in secret. She'd seen that whole conversation with Mina.

A COOL PRESENT

"Heh heh! You know how to lay it on, Rei Rei. A 'present,' eh? I thought I'd get a cavity from how sweet that was!" Paula began reciting my conversation with Mina. "'I'm looking forward to it!' 'You better be!' Whew—it's getting hot in here! Just *describing* this is embarrassing!"

She added the exchange about the refrigerator to her repertoire of stories to tease me with.

DRUGSTORE IN ANOTHER WORLD
~ The Slow Life of a Cheat Pharmacist ~

5

The Friendly, Totally-Not-Scary Neighborhood Goblin

Mornings were chilly these days, but at the same time, the air was fresh. As I prepared to open the drugstore, I heard Mina making breakfast in the back.

"Nice and peaceful," I murmured.

As I appreciated this refreshing morning, Vivi popped in. "Good morning, Reiji!"

Oh, right. Vivi and Ejil are working today. "Hey. Morning."

"Gyah gyah!"

I jumped. "What the heck was that?"

"Wha—you followed me?! I told you not to!" Vivi exclaimed.

"Gyah gyah?"

Vivi turned her back to me, crouching.

"Hey, what was that weird noise, Vivi?" I peeked over her shoulder to see a light-green humanoid creature with a wrinkled face and yellow eyes.

GOBLIN: Small monster. Lives in fields and wooded areas.

"What the hell?!" I cried. "A g-goblin?! What're you doing, bringing a monster in here?!" I'd been in this world for some time, so I'd seen all kinds of creatures from afar in the woods and mountains. Still, I'd never seen a monster up close like this.

I distanced myself from the strange pair. "W-we gotta call Annabelle!" It was nothing to be proud of, but I could barely have squared off with a small dog. Against anything bigger or fiercer than that, I was doomed.

"No, wait!" Vivi cried. "The goblin followed me here by accident! I'll take it outside town, all right? I won't let it do anything bad!"

"Really? I mean, are you okay? Isn't it dangerous?" I met the goblin's eyes.

"Gyah!" it shrieked.

Eek! Jeez, that thing scares the hell out of me. If I'm close, it'll probably try to bite me.

"Well, humans originally worshipped me, and monsters see me the same way," Vivi said.

THE FRIENDLY...NEIGHBORHOOD GOBLIN

I guess even goblins worship spirits.

"This little one's been all alone for a while," she continued. "I think it got separated from its pack. It loves the lake; it basically follows me around now. I told it to stay by the water, but..."

Vivi apparently hadn't noticed the goblin's presence as she arrived in Kalta. It probably got in through a hole in the town walls, like a dog or cat. It was still early morning, so not many folks were outside; that explained how it reached the drugstore without causing chaos.

"I know you say you'll take it out of town, but if the gatekeepers catch you, it'll be a pain," I warned Vivi. "They'll punish you too."

I wonder what it'd take to turn around Vivi's bad luck.

"Eek! What should I do?"

"Even if you take the goblin outside town, won't it just try to get back in? It found its way here without using the gate," I pointed out. "Look, you can go home for today. We won't be busy, and we should get rid of that thing."

What I'd said clearly upset Vivi. She teared up. "I-I get it. You're firing me for good this time! Working here three days of week was something I looked forward to!"

She looks forward to working at the drugstore? That's definitely the kind of line you'd want other introverts to overhear. I tilted my head. *However you slice it, it'll be a huge mess if townsfolk see Vivi with that goblin. What's the plan?*

A magic circle suddenly appeared in the air, and Ejil showed up, flowing cape and all. "Good morning, Doctor! Thank you for going out of your way to greet me at the door!" He lowered his head as if groveling.

"Morning, Ejil. Perfect timing. Can you do something about him?" I pointed.

"Him?" Ejil gazed at the goblin beside the lake spirit. "Good morning, Vivi. Is that your pet?"

"Hi. No, um, it followed me on its own."

"Gyah gyah!" The goblin stared at Ejil. As I'd expected, it was terrified of the demon king.

"What'd it say, Ejil?"

"Beats me."

"Uh...you mean, your powers don't allow you to understand it?" If two demons spoke different languages, they could communicate using thought transference, as long as both were higher beings.

"Thought transference doesn't work with a goblin—not even for a demon king—unless you're also a goblin," Ejil explained. "Goblins aren't intelligent, so they don't possess a language other races understand." That was the reason humans couldn't perform thought transference with dogs, he added.

THE FRIENDLY...NEIGHBORHOOD GOBLIN

"Hunh. Really?" If this goblin were a dog or cat, the drugstore could've kept it as a pet. Unfortunately, it was a monster, and Kirio Drugs was a business.

"I can turn this thing into dust instantaneously, Doctor. I am the demon king, after all," Ejil declared, cackling like the edgelord he was. "This is the perfect chance to show off my power!"

"N-no, don't!" Vivi shrieked. "That'd be too awful! The poor thing just got separated from its pack."

"Gyah! Gyah gyah!"

I had no clue what the goblin was saying, but I agreed with Vivi. "Yeah, no. Not happening, Ejil. There'll be no murders around the drugstore."

"I could always use teleportation magic to take it to some mountain," Ejil offered.

That might be the best option.

"Either way, Doctor, this goblin will stay alone if it can't reunite with its pack," the demon king added. "Believe it or not, goblins have strong communities. They always treat outsiders as outsiders."

That's terrible. It's just like how transfer students are always considered transfer students, and can't settle in with the rest of their class, I reflected. *It might not be my problem, but...*

Vivi waved. "Do you think this little one *wants* to

search for its pack, Reiji? It refuses to leave my lake. I figured it'd go on its own if it wanted to."

Makes sense.

Just then, my medicine-making skill activated, informing me of necessary ingredients and steps. "Ah," I whispered. Ejil and Vivi looked at me. "Looks like I can whip something up. I'm gonna need your help, Ejil. Come with me."

"Yes, sir!" replied the demon king enthusiastically, following me toward the lab.

"Um, what's my job, Reiji?" Vivi asked.

"Make sure no one catches that little goblin while I concoct this new product."

"O-okay! I'll do my best."

"Much obliged," I yawned, entering the lab with Ejil.

Noticing us, Mina popped her head in. "Breakfast is ready, Mr. Reiji."

"Save our meals for later, woman! The good doctor is making a brand-new product, and he specifically asked for *my* assistance!" The demon king grinned proudly right before I gave the crown of his head a fierce smack. "Owie!"

"Mina is not *'woman.'* Why're you always such a jerk to her?"

The "woman" in question simply giggled. "It's fine, Mr. Reiji. I'm sure the demon king business has stressed Ejil out terribly," she said, leaving the lab.

THE FRIENDLY...NEIGHBORHOOD GOBLIN

The demon king "business"? Since when is that a business?

"Hmph. As though that woman understands anything," Ejil said pompously.

I smacked my helper's head again. With his assistance, though, I made smooth progress on my new creation.

> **TRANSLATOR DX (LEMON FLAVOR):** Enables communication in other races' languages. Easy-to-drink lemon flavor.

Ejil's eyes sparkled as he looked at the glowing liquid. "You're all finished, Doctor?"

"Yup. We'll be able to understand that goblin now."

I took a sip, discovering that the translator DX basically tasted like lemonade. *It's really good, actually. Hmm... no side effects, as far as I can tell.*

Several customers had swung by; I asked Noela and Ejil to handle them while I looked for Vivi and the goblin. The pair were in the living room. "What're you doing in here?"

"Ah, Reiji! Customers came in, so I thought we'd hide in the house," Vivi explained. "What'd you end up making?"

I explained the new concoction and had her take a sip.

"Ooh!" she exclaimed. "This's tasty."

"I'm thrilled that you're fond of it, Lady Vivi."

"Huh? What'd you say, Reiji?"

"That wasn't me. I'd never call you 'Lady Vivi.'"

"Right..."

It couldn't be...

The lake spirit and I slowly looked at the goblin.

"It would seem you finally understand me," it stated.

"We understand the goblin?!" we shrieked. As we heard its grunts, we simultaneously heard a coherent "voice-over." The goblin's voice was astoundingly gruff, like some veteran warrior's.

"L-let's calm down, Vivi," I stammered. "Remember, we drank a potion that enabled thought transference."

"O-oh, yeah."

Trying to collect myself, I cleared my throat, then simply told the goblin my name.

"Sir Reiji, correct?" it repeated. "I have no name. Call me whatever you wish."

Since the goblin made "gyah" sounds, and struck me as male, I went with "Gyao."

"What happened to your pack?" I asked Gyao. "Were you separated from them?"

Gyao sat cross-legged. "I wasn't separated from my pack. I left them."

"But why would you do that? Aren't you lonely?" Vivi asked, concerned.

THE FRIENDLY...NEIGHBORHOOD GOBLIN

Gyao laughed in a deep, low voice, shaking his head. "I found a master I wished to devote my life to. Thus, I am not remotely lonely."

His voice almost makes him sound valiant, I thought.

"Ah, that's cool," replied Vivi. "I...I totally get how you feel. I serve Reiji as my master. Three times a week, anyway."

She realizes he's talking about her, *right?* Ignoring Vivi's completely off-base comparison, I explained the situation to Gyao. "Look, according to human rules, monsters that enter town are executed immediately."

"I fully understand that. However, since my master made her way here, she needed protection."

"In short, you're here as Vivi's bodyguard?"

"Precisely." Gyao nodded deeply.

"There you have it, Vivi."

"But, um...that might be a problem," Vivi objected. "First of all, I don't need a bodyguard or underling."

"My word!" Gyao yelped.

I thought maybe she'd beat around the bush, but no, she went straight for the jugular.

"As a spirit, Lady Vivi, you naturally spend most of your time at your shrine," Gyao argued. "Upon seeing you, I felt it was my mission in life to protect such a fragile being!"

"This is getting too depressing for me, Reiji." Vivi sighed.

"C'mon, don't say that in front of him," I whispered, glancing at Gyao. His eyes were now devoid of their earlier luster.

I get that it's a pain that he randomly appointed Vivi his master, then made himself her bodyguard. Still, she could've been gentler.

Since Gyao had already abandoned his pack, there was no turning back for him. If he'd been here to cause trouble, chasing him off would've been easy. However, he was acting out of loyalty to Vivi, which made him extra difficult to deal with.

"Uh—I have an idea!" I cried, turning to Gyao. "When Vivi's in town, I'll take responsibility for protecting her. It's my job as her master to watch over her anyhow. When she's at the lake, though, you handle it. How's that sound?"

That was no sweat, since Vivi wasn't in danger at the drugstore. As long as Gyao didn't come into Kalta, there'd be no issues.

"Hmm." Gyao bowed his head once more, satisfied. "I leave my master in your capable hands, Sir Reiji."

"No problem." I turned to Vivi. "Got it? When you're not in town, Gyao here will accompany you. Wicked, huh? No more feeling lonely!"

THE FRIENDLY...NEIGHBORHOOD GOBLIN

"Y-yeah..." Vivi's expression was, well, something. She definitely didn't seem thrilled.

"I shall excuse myself, Master, and await you at home." Gyao bowed to Vivi.

I showed him to the back exit, saw him off, and rejoined Vivi in the drugstore.

"I don't want to go back to the lake today, Reiji!" She was on the verge of tears.

I patted her back, flashing the biggest smile I could muster. "No big deal!"

"Augh! You're enjoying this, aren't you?! I can tell by that expression! You're hoping something funny happens!" Vivi snapped. "Urgh. That goblin's too melodramatic for me."

"Just look at this as having a new friend."

"I'll try my best."

That was how Vivi acquired a goblin companion.

Although it didn't always work, the new translator DX seemed to allow all kinds of species to understand us. I couldn't wait to try talking to another monster—or even a dog or cat. Just like that, I gained something else to look forward to every day.

DRUGSTORE in another world
~ The Slow Life of a Cheat Pharmacist ~

Children Are Merciless

"YOU KNOW, I really think I lack dignity," Vivi remarked as we watched the store.

"I mean, do you really *need* it?"

"Of course! I'm a spirit. If I had a more dignified aura, people wouldn't underestimate me so often." She looked somber. I wasn't sure how to reply.

I guessed that Vivi was saying this because, three days ago, some neighborhood kids had swung by while she watched the store. They'd bullied her, teased her, and basically just given her grief. She made the perfect prey, since she was always pessimistic and wore her heart on her sleeve. *Hell, if I were a kid, I'd probably pick on Vivi too.*

I'd eventually managed to chase the kids away. By that point, though, Vivi was already on the verge of tears.

I sighed. "How about astounding people with some advanced magic, since you're a spirit and all?"

"I can't use that magic unless I'm at the lake."

"Hunh. But you *can* use astounding magic? What kind?"

Vivi giggled. "Spells that human mages only dream of using!"

"Whoa! Now you sound all-powerful."

"For instance, my magic purifies the lake water!"

I hesitated. "Man...where're all the customers?"

"Why did you just ignore what I said about the lake water?" Vivi pulled my sleeve, annoyed. "It's safe to drink for animals, monsters, and humans! The fish are peppy every day! There probably isn't a lake like that anywhere else in the world! I'm amazing, right? Hey!"

"Look, could you give me some space? Your hand's pretty cold."

"Oh, sorry. Wait—hey! You're a jerk!"

"How come? You're a lake spirit, so you have to stay cool or you can't retain your human form, right?"

"That's not what I meant! Couldn't you, like, react? Ask questions about my magic! I'm up for answering anything! Oh—wait, I get it. You're hiding how surprised you are!" Vivi kept boasting about her lame lake magic, grinning.

CHILDREN ARE MERCILESS

If her magic just filters the lake, she can kiss "dignity" goodbye. "You're coming off as kind of desperate, Vivi."

"Don't sneer at me! Yes, I'm desperate, okay?! I don't want kids to bully me anymore!"

"Hmm. Let's set the whole 'magic' thing aside for now, then."

"Huh? Why?!"

"Hmm. How about an ace up your sleeve...?" I mumbled, brainstorming.

My words seemed to trigger something in the unfortunate spirit's brain. She gazed at me respectfully. *Yup, her eyes are pure and innocent. Sparkling, even. And her magic won't help, so a trump card would be handy.*

"Let's approach this whole 'dignity' thing from a different angle," I suggested. "How about giving off an aura that makes you *unapproachable*?"

Vivi apparently drew a blank. "What do you mean?"

Okay, give her an example she can work with. "You know how it's hard to talk to someone who looks cranky?"

Vivi nodded. "My aura will be more dignified if I'm grumpy?"

Hrm, not quite. Still, that might work against the kids. "Just keep telling yourself you're an all-powerful spirit. You're so strong, you could blow away any human with just a breath, and some idiot's polluting your lake!"

Vivi growled. "I'm *so* pissed off!"

Mina popped her head into the drugstore. "I'm about to make lunch, Vivi. Would you care to help? A while ago, you said you wanted to try cooking."

"Who cares about cooking?! I'm fed up! Why the hell did that fool dirty my lake?!"

"All right. I'll take that as a no." Mina smiled awkwardly and retreated.

Vivi gaped at the spot where she'd been, then turned to me. "Reiji..."

"Yeah?"

"I think I just slipped up."

She had; she'd lost her unapproachable aura. "I had the same thought. What a coincidence."

"It's not a coincidence!" Vivi smacked me lightly, sending a chill up my arm. "I bet that grumpy aura upset Mina!"

"Well, how about we try changing your look instead?"

"I should grow a beard!" she exclaimed.

I tried to imagine it. "Uh...that's not working for me. A beard would come off as a joke—like you were wearing a disguise."

"Then how about making myself taller?!"

"Oh! That might actually work. You'd seem *intimidating*, rather than dignified." I got behind Vivi and stuck my head between her legs. Holding her thighs, I lifted her upward.

"Whoa! Wh-what're you doing?!"

"Feel taller?"

"Oh, gosh! I'm so high up. I *am* taller! Tee hee! Wait, this isn't more dignified—it's just fun!"

"Isn't that good enough?"

"We're shooting for intimidating, Reiji! Sitting on your shoulders doesn't make *me* taller. Come on—prescribe me something for height!"

"That's too much hassle."

"Don't be like that! I'm your employee! Are you really okay with a bunch of kids bullying me? You told Gyao you'd protect me, right?" Vivi yanked at my hair.

"Ow, ow! Okay, fine, I get it! I'll make you something! Stop!" I immediately put her down. I could tell she'd keep lashing out if I didn't help.

"I'm counting on you!" Vivi bowed her head.

"I guess I have no choice," I grumbled to myself, heading for the lab. Spotting Mina, I told her what'd just transpired.

Time to get down to business.

An extra thirty centimeters would change Vivi's image. The formula wasn't too difficult, so I finished quickly.

BIGGER BIGGEST: Enlarges body. Growth depends on amount consumed.

This is almost like doping. Anyhow, prescribing Vivi one dose of the bigger-biggest treatment should scare those brats into submission.

"Yo, Vivi! I'm done!" I called, returning to the shop. I found her dealing with customers—five kids, in fact.

"Ew! Negative Nancy's working again!" one shrieked.

"What're you doing, lady?"

"You sure seem bored!"

"Why're you so whiny all the time?"

"You'll never make friends acting like that, wimp!"

The kids had only just entered, but Vivi was already holding back large tears. "I-I'm in the middle of work! Go home!"

Damn, she's weepy. Still, I can't blame her if they bully her like this.

"Hey, brats!" I snapped. "Show her some respect! I'll have you know a Negative Nancy can be damn popular with customers! We don't sell candy here—get your butts home!"

"Shut up, old man!"

Excuse me?! I cracked my knuckles. "I'll have to show you brats what happens when you mess with an angry

CHILDREN ARE MERCILESS

geezer!" The kids screeched and rushed out. Sighing, I headed back to the counter. "Dumb brats."

"Thanks for saving me, Reiji."

"No big. You do realize they pick on you because you don't have your guard up, right? Anyhow..." I handed her the bigger-biggest liquid. "This should make you taller."

She gazed at it happily. "If I drink this, they won't bug me anymore?"

If Vivi was still thin-skinned once she was taller, the kids might continue to tease her. But if her body grew, maybe her attitude would change too.

Vivi popped the cap off the bottle, downing the formula in one go. "Whew! Yum!"

"Whoa, wait!" *She drank it all before I could explain anything!* I watched Vivi rapidly grow taller.

"Huh? Whoa! I'm growing!"

Thonk! Her head smacked the ceiling three meters up. "Owie!"

She stopped growing at that point, but her body was several times taller and wider. I actually had to look up to see her face. *She's huge. She changed from spirit to titan!*

"H-how're you feeling?"

"Incredible! I can see so much more!"

Fortunately, her clothes had grown with her; she was totally covered. However... "Uh, Vivi...this's kinda hard to say, but…"

"What?" She looked down at me.

"No matter where I stand, I can see your underwear."

"Eek! Don't look!" Vivi immediately crouched; her knees and elbows brushed the shelves, and one bottle after another fell to the floor.

"Whoa! Hold up! Go outside for now! You're too big for the drugstore!"

"Gosh, I'm sorry!" Holding her skirt hem modestly, Vivi glanced at me. "Don't you dare look!"

She slowly exited. Of course, as she did so, her butt faced me, and she exposed herself completely. *Sigh.* It wasn't a big deal; her panties were bigger, and honestly, they just looked like a huge blanket. *Kinda hard to feel anything about an enormous bedsheet.*

"AAAH! A GIANTESS!"

Hearing children's screams, I rushed outside. The brats from earlier were pointing and yelling at Vivi.

Yeah, she's sure big. She's about as tall as a two-story house.

"Heh heh! How do you like me now?" Vivi shrieked. "If you mess with me again, I'll forehead-flick you into oblivion!"

Her tone had changed. *I guess the extra height did help. You've grown, Vivi. Physically, anyhow.* Vivi had begun her counterattack in earnest—or so I thought.

CHILDREN ARE MERCILESS

"We gotta protect our town!" one child squealed.

"Yeah!"

"Split up!"

"Aye aye!"

The kids surrounded Vivi. As they flitted about, she seemed lost. "Huh? What's going on?"

They whipped out small wooden swords. "Attack!"

"Yaaaah!" They struck at Vivi's legs.

"W-wait! Stop! That stings!"

"This is our town!"

Seeing the brave kids protect Kalta from the titan, I found myself moved. *This town's future is safe and sound.*

One kid looked upward. "Whoa! I can see her panties!"

"Hey, don't look!" Vivi pressed her skirt down.

It was too late. Like the piranhas of the Amazon River, the kids smelled blood.

"Even her panties are huge!" one squealed.

"Miss Big-Panties!"

"Why're your panties black?"

"Eaugh! She pooped herself!"

"Ain't you too old to do that?"

The lake spirit was wearing dark underwear, so the kids had gotten the wrong idea. "She pooped herself! She pooped herself! She pooped herself!" they chanted, clapping along.

Talk about devastating psychological warfare. These kids are vicious.

"I *didn't* poop myself!" Vivi shrieked in embarrassment.

My ears rang; I covered them instinctively while the kids laughed their asses off at Vivi's volume.

She crouched, sobbing. Bucket-sized tears fell to the ground one after another, producing a small river.

Hunh. I feel like I watched something exactly like this back in grade school.

"Aren't you supposed to be grown up? Why're you crying like a baby?!"

"What're you crying about, Miss Big-Panties?"

"Why're your panties that color?"

Vivi hadn't stopped bawling.

"This is boring. Let's go home."

"We'll be back later!"

The kids left, tired of Vivi. The poor lake spirit was all choked up, her eyes completely bloodshot.

"I honestly think they just want you to play with them," I told her.

I figured it was similar to a kid teasing a kid they liked. Children didn't pay attention to people they didn't want to deal with.

"Even if that's true, I hate it!"

CHILDREN ARE MERCILESS

The bigger-biggest liquid's effects wore off, returning Vivi to her normal height. I stroked her head gently.

"Look, next time they come by, try playing. We always chase them off, so they're mad, and they get back at us." Sure, we could've just scared the kids away for good, but that would've been tough for Vivi. "Operation Friendship, got it? If being strict isn't working, let loose a little. Who knows, it might work out."

"That...could be fun." Vivi giggled, and I smiled back at her.

◆●◆

A few days later, the kids came by the drugstore while Vivi was working. She extended an olive branch, and they played together. It sounded like they had a lot of fun.

When I thought about it, the kids only showed up during Vivi's shifts. I was sure they saw her as one of the neighborhood's older girls; I totally understood why they wanted her attention.

Despite that happy ending, wimpy Vivi still didn't like being underestimated. "Reiji, I want to be more dignified!"

DRUGSTORE in another world
~ The Slow Life of a Cheat Pharmacist ~

Chocolate Day

"You know Chocolate Day's coming up, right, Reiji?"

Zeral was here to hang out. On the other side of the counter, he put his chin in his hands, looking melancholy.

"What's that?"

"You seriously don't know? Every year, you give people chocolate and confess feelings you otherwise couldn't."

Sounds like Chocolate Day is basically just Valentine's Day.

The young lord across from me had a girlfriend—Feris. She was kind of unhinged, but she'd probably bring him chocolate.

Thunk! I kicked Zeral's shin.

He completely ignored my envious blow. "Listen, man," he said with a sigh. "Feris is all excited to bring me homemade chocolate."

Seriously? He's bragging? "Great. Wonderful. Fabulous."

"But she's the daughter of a good family from outside Kalta. She's never actually *made* chocolate before. You reading between the lines, buddy?"

"I'll prescribe you some stomach medicine, okay? After eating Feris's chocolate, make sure you take it."

"Er…I mean, that'd be great and all, but I'd prefer a better solution!" Zeral whined pathetically, flattening himself on the counter.

I grabbed a bottle of stomach medicine off the shelf and put it on the counter as well. "It's the *perfect* solution. Aren't you worried about how you'll feel after eating your girlfriend's awful chocolate?"

"I mean, that does concern me, but I've still got some stomach meds around. It's okay." He quietly pushed the bottle back toward me. "I want to be able to *enjoy* Feris's chocolate."

"Impossible. Besides, why does the recipient have to worry about this gift?"

Zeral pressed his forehead into the counter. "I wear my heart on my sleeve. Even if I say 'They're delicious!' Feris will know I'm bluffing as soon as she looks at my face."

"On the other hand," I said, "if she figures that out, she might be like 'Oh, gosh! My chocolate's *that* awful? I'll work extra hard to learn to make it for you!'"

CHOCOLATE DAY

Heck, if that was how things went down, she'd at least seem loving, regardless of her cooking talent.

That was apparently unlikely. "If only! Feris cooked for me once before, and I lied and told her it was delicious. Unfortunately, she saw right through me and lost her temper. She was all 'Why don't you like it?!'"

As usual, Feris and Zeral were major pains in the ass, although—as a third party—seeing them at odds was kind of entertaining. "You *do* realize a dude with no girlfriend would usually end this conversation and tell you not to be a greedy asshole?"

"C'mon, bud. Don't be like that. She was like 'You hate my cooking because you're eating some other woman's food!'"

"She flipped her lid?"

"Yup. If that were all, it would've been fine, but then she started swinging a knife around. Let me tell you, her knife skills are improving a *lot*."

Ah, I get it. He wants to enjoy the chocolate because he's gonna be on thin ice. Feris was definitely beautiful, but I couldn't help picturing her with a dark aura. *She smells like danger...mortal danger.*

"I do feel for you, man," I admitted. "Maybe Mina could teach Feris to cook or something."

"That'd be cool and all, but it wouldn't help much if

Feris couldn't remember any of her advice." Zeral sighed. "If things continue like this, I'm going to die, Reiji."

"That's true of everyone."

"Aren't we supposed to be friends?" Near tears, Zeral wriggled on the counter like a slug. "Help me!"

I sighed and gave up. "Fine. I'll go see if I can whip up something."

"Woo!" He high-fived me. "You're my BFF!"

"Woo!" I echoed. "Same." *What the hell's wrong with us?* "I want you to watch the store in exchange, though. If customers come by, grab me from the lab."

"You got it, Boss! Wait—where're Mina and Noela?"

"They left for the Rabbit Tavern before noon. They won't be back until tonight." Elaine had come by the drugstore this morning, and the three girls left together; they'd said something about helping at the tavern, although I thought it was closed today.

"Now that you mention it, I saw Paula and that merc lady on my way here," Zeral noted. "Oh, and that elf girl too. Ah...I get what's going on."

"I guess the ladies planned a get-together. What're you grinning about?"

"Oh, nothing. Good for you, bud."

What the hell's he talking about? "Yeah, good for me... or something," I mumbled, bewildered. *Paula, Annabelle, and Ririka are at the Rabbit Tavern too? Did they rent it out for a party or something? Nice.*

I still had no clue what the deal was, but I made my way into the lab. "A product that'll help Zeral enjoy Feris's chocolate, eh?"

Folding my arms, I scratched my chin in a classic thinking pose. *The problem is, everyone likes different things. It's totally possible that Feris's cooking isn't actually awful—Zeral just doesn't like it.* Still, if he'd asked me to try it, I would've turned down the sample faster than the speed of light.

"Hmm...Zeral did say he wears his heart on his sleeve." The moment I remembered that, my medicine-making skill reacted. *Great. Once I formulate this, maybe Feris won't swing knives around anymore.*

After finishing up, I carried the new treatment into the drugstore. "This ain't gonna make Feris's chocolate taste good, Zeral. Got it?"

He nodded. After we got on the same page about that, I explained the treatment. Despite my opening statement, Zeral seemed happy with my results. "Thanks, bud! Now I don't have to worry about getting stabbed!"

Well, he should still generally watch his back. Feris is, uh... scary. I waved goodbye as Zeral headed off. *I should've given him more stomach meds.*

It got dark. As I closed the drugstore, Mina and Noela returned.

"Home, Master!"

"We're back! Sorry for being gone all day, Mr. Reiji."

"No need to apologize. Nice to see you. How was your party?"

Upon inspection, I noticed that both girls held paper bags. Had the kind Rabbit Tavern staff given them goodies?

"Master! Master!" Noela was on the verge of saying something.

"Noela, stop!" Mina covered her mouth. "How many times did I tell you to keep that secret today? You can talk as much as you like tomorrow, all right?"

"Garrooooo! Noela forgot!"

Mina turned back to me. "Um…er…the party was loads of fun."

They were hiding something, but apparently, they'd tell me what was up tomorrow. I opted not to pry deeper.

Noela was squirming like crazy; just before she reopened her mouth, she snapped to her senses, shaking her head over and over. *Man, Noela really wants to spill the beans.*

◆◆◆

CHOCOLATE DAY

The next morning, I awoke to my mattress shaking violently. "E-earthquake?!"

No—Noela had just crawled onto my bed. "Morning, Master!" She held a box with a ribbon bow. "Noela grateful!"

"Uh...what's going on?"

Before my eyes, Noela unwrapped the box, taking out some chocolate. "Eat, Master!"

She forced the confection into my mouth. *Smoosh!*

"Noela make! Yummy?!"

Ah! Today's Chocolate Day. Duh. She'd absolutely stuffed my mouth with chocolate, but it quickly melted. "Wow. That's pretty tasty!"

"Garrooo!" Noela hugged me tightly, wagging her tail.

As we prepared to open the drugstore, I heard a horse-drawn carriage outside. Its door opened to reveal Elaine, as I expected.

"Sir Reiji! Noela! I've arrived." Elaine brushed one of her drill-like ringlets off her shoulder. "Good day to you both."

"Yo, Elaine."

"Morning!"

"Um, S-Sir Reiji, could you please come here?" Elaine returned to her carriage, beckoning me.

Curious, I climbed inside the carriage; Noela followed after me. "Not you, Noela."

"Arroo." Looking irritated, she headed back to the store.

I sat across from Elaine, as she directed. "What's up? You're here early."

"W-well, I've never given a man besides Father anything before, so forgive me if I'm awkward." Elaine held a small box. "Um...please accept these. I-I don't know whether they're any good, but I made them myself, just for you...whom I admire so deeply."

"Oh, wow. Thanks." *I wondered why she seemed so on edge. Guess it's because she made me chocolate.*

"I do hope you enjoy them."

"Thanks. I'm sure they're delicious."

Elaine closed her eyes. "Mother, Father, please forgive your shameless daughter." She pursed her lips slightly. "Sir Reiji..."

"Hrm?" Glancing outside the carriage, I saw that Noela hadn't opened the drugstore yet. *Gah! She's skipping work. Where'd she go?*

I quickly exited the vehicle, telling the elderly driver that Elaine had finished her errand, although her eyes were still closed. *Smack!* The driver cracked his whip, and the horses began to canter.

As the carriage rolled away, I heard Elaine shriek, "This isn't the Chocolate Day I had in mind!"

CHOCOLATE DAY

After that episode, I wound up receiving chocolate from Paula, Annabelle, Ririka, and even Rena, the Rabbit Tavern's barmaid. It was quite a barrage, considering that I'd only ever gotten chocolate from my mom up till that day.

As the sun set, Zeral swung by. "Reiji! Pal!"

"Yeah, that's me. What's up, buddy?"

Zeral raised his hand enthusiastically. I did likewise, and we high-fived. We'd gotten into the habit of that little greeting.

"You used that prescription, right?" I asked. "It should've kept Feris's chocolate from grossing you out, if nothing else."

"It was perfect! It worked just like you said." Zeral shook my hand, then showed me a half-empty vial—the formula I'd made yesterday.

> CREAM: Dulls palate by impacting senses of smell and touch.

At the end of the day, Zeral only wanted to enjoy Feris's chocolate so that she wouldn't catch him in a lie and get mad. The thing was, since everyone had a different idea of what was tasty, creating a product that made everything delicious was tough.

Therefore, I needed to keep Zeral from tasting "bad" flavors. *Of course, the downside is that he can't taste "good" flavors either, but eh.*

"Good," I replied. "I'm glad she didn't stab you."

"Don't even joke! I was serious about that. Luckily, Feris seems to realize that she's not exactly accustomed to cooking. She says she wants to get better."

"And you'll be her taste tester?"

"Ha ha! Yup. Next time, though, I'm gonna eat what she cooks *without* the cream. Drinking that is rude to her. Besides, how else can I tell whether she improves?"

"People like you go down first on the battlefield."

"Don't be like that! Anyway, I really owe you one."

"Let me guess," I sighed. "After you ate her chocolate, I bet you two got all cuddly?"

"Ha ha! How'd you know?"

"Go home, you damn lovebird!"

Zeral thanked me one more time, laughing, then headed out.

Bleh. Romantics like him unintentionally put guys like me to shame.

I chilled out and watched the store as I snacked on the chocolate I'd received.

Eventually, Mina poked her head in. "Do you have some spare time, Mr. Reiji?"

CHOCOLATE DAY

"Hm? Of course."

"You take such good care of me daily. I know it's Chocolate Day, but to say thanks, I made you this instead." Mina presented me with two slices of roll cake on a plate. "I know you've eaten lots of sweets today, but I hope you enjoy it. Oh—and I've got leftovers, so if it's good, come have as much as you like. Once Noela finds it, I doubt there'll be any left."

"Ha ha! Thanks." I plunged my fork into a slice and took a bite. The cake was super light, and the frosting's sweetness was perfect. "You're one hell of a baker, Mina. This is delicious." I almost felt like I could eat that cake forever. "So did all the girls head to the tavern yesterday to prep for Chocolate Day?"

"You figured that out?"

"It explains why everyone's chocolate was so good." Mina must've kept an eye on the other girls while they made the treats. She smiled warmly, watching me eat. *Am I really that fun to look at?*

"I'll pour you some tea," she said, leaving for the kitchen.

Aw. I should've asked for another slice.

"Oh, no! Noela, I made that for Mr. Reiji! Why'd you eat it all?!"

"W-wasn't me. Noela no eat!"

"You have frosting on your mouth!"

"Arroo?!"

Hearing the conversation, I couldn't help laughing and digging into some more chocolate. It really was weird how just eating sweets made you feel so happy and fulfilled. Getting chocolate from someone was wonderful; it honestly didn't matter whether it was a romantic gift.

"Man, chocolate sure is delish." *I'll have to make sure to give all the girls something in return.*

I ended up eating way too much of the stuff, killing my appetite for dinner. Needless to say, that didn't make Mina too happy.

Eventually, I stocked the cream alongside the drugstore's cold medicine, which I'd heard was too bitter for children. The combination was perfect, and the cream wound up being popular with mothers whose kids wouldn't take medicine.

8

Colds Aren't Caught Out of Nowhere

EJIL WAS COUGHING up a storm.

Did he catch a cold or something?

Resting my chin in my hands on the store counter, I shot that question at Ejil, who was dusting the shelves. "You're the demon king, and you catch colds?"

"What are 'colds,' Doctor?"

"A type of illness."

"I see." Ejil's expression turned serious. "Every year, when the weather gets chilly, I cough like this. My body gets heavy, and I'm sometimes feverish. The humans must've developed some awful, dirty biological weapon to use against me."

"Nah. You just have a cold."

"But worry not, Doctor!" Ejil continued. "If I rest for a few days, I'll recover fully."

He sneezed. His gaze was unfocused, and his face was ruddy. There were no thermometers in this world, though. Besides, would a demon king run a fever like a human?

He should just have rested at his castle. "You can go home for today if you don't feel great, Ejil."

"N-no way! I'm eager for my encounter with Noela."

"When has that ever actually worked out for you?"

"Don't you understand just how much I look forward to my shifts every week, Doctor?!"

Nevertheless, Ejil coughed and coughed. I was pretty sure even I could've defeated him in his current state. His red face turned pale, and his teeth chattered.

"D-Doctor, aren't you cold?" he mumbled.

"You're getting chills because you're sick. Like I said, you can go home early."

"L-let me at least tell Noela I'm leaving." Ejil wobbled away.

I grabbed his shoulder. "No need. I'll let her know. It'd suck if Noela or Mina caught your cold."

"Ugh! I feel like a fool, caving to a bioweapon concocted by mere humans!" Ejil began to cry.

I guess being sick makes him especially tenderhearted.

"Why're you crying?" I forced a laugh, then handed him some cold meds and an energy potion from the shelf. "Go home and take care of yourself, got it?"

COLDS AREN'T CAUGHT OUT OF NOWHERE

"Your prescriptions are as powerful as a million soldiers!" Ejil declared. "I'll recover soon. It'd affect my army's morale if their king succumbed to an illness!"

Ejil bowed his head, then headed home. I watched him leave, exasperated. His cape usually billowed proudly, but today, it was just kind of...blowing.

The drugstore carries cold medicine, but not anything for cold prevention, I realized. "I should make something. It'd be bad if everybody caught a bug."

Wait a sec. Out of everyone who works here, I'm the only human. A werewolf, a ghost, the demon king, a spirit... Variety is the spice of life.

Still, even non-humans got sick in this world. Mina had been bedridden for a while, and Ejil was clearly ill. Leaving the store to Noela, I got to work in the lab.

> **GARAPPE:** Mouthwash and disinfectant. Prevents bad breath.

"Gargling with this should more than prevent colds."

Satisfied, I carried the mouthwash to the bathroom and called in Noela and Mina.

"What up, Master?"

"What're you doing, Mr. Reiji?"

"I made some mouthwash!" I presented the bottle

theatrically. The girls gave me no reaction whatsoever. "Mouthwash, ladies. Understand?"

"Mouthwash?" they repeated, tilting their heads.

"Noela no know 'mouthwash,' Master."

Mina nodded. "If you say it's some sort of medicine, Mr. Reiji, I believe you. But..."

"Wait, for real? It's just mouthwash! The kind you gargle with!"

The pair blinked at me, looked at each other, then shook their heads. *They really don't get it.*

"Well, anyway, using this stuff keeps you from getting sick."

It'd be fastest to show them. I poured a trickle of mouthwash into a cup, diluting it with some water. Then I dumped the liquid into my mouth, gargled, and spat it out.

"Um, Mr. Reiji, it's rude to spit out your drink."

"Nah. You're supposed to use mouthwash like that."

"Noela! Noela!" The werewolf girl hopped up and down, her hand raised. "Noela no get colds!"

"That's held true so far, but who knows about the future? Colds suck, Noela," I warned her.

"Garoo! They do?!"

"So, this 'mouthwash' deters colds?"

The girls seemed to catch on at last.

COLDS AREN'T CAUGHT OUT OF NOWHERE

Next up was a quick lesson on how to gargle. The three of us harmonized. Mina and I spat the mouthwash out, but Noela's mouth was entirely empty.

"Er, Noela, did you spit out that mouthwash?"

"Gulped."

"You're not supposed to swallow it!"

Having explained mouthwash's importance, I told the girls to ensure they always used it when they got home.

When the drugstore starts selling this, I should probably attach instructions, since people in Kalta are unfamiliar with it. With that thought, I abruptly coughed. *In retrospect, I felt kind of sluggish the whole time I was in the lab.*

I coughed again. *Wait...I'm a little dizzy. Could I have caught a cold?* Mouthwash deterred viruses, so I must've gotten it in the drugstore. *That damn demon king passed it on to me!*

"You're rather flushed, Mr. Reiji. Are you all right?" Mina was right in front of me, yet her voice sounded far away. She put her chilly hand on my forehead.

I only remembered what happened after that in bits and pieces. I was pretty sure Mina put me to bed; when I woke up, it was nighttime.

Ugh...my body's so heavy. My head hurts. My throat hurts. This isn't just a little bug—it's the real deal. Damn you, Ejil! Even your colds are demonic and over the top.

"Master awake!" Noela was in bed with me. I'd thought it was oddly warm in here.

"Go sleep in another room, Noela. You'll catch my cold."

"Master look cold! Noela warm up."

Talking was too much struggle; I simply stroked Noela's head. Eventually, she crawled out of bed and left me in peace. *To be honest, I'm kinda lonely now.* A minute later, I heard the girls talking outside.

"Noela give to Master!"

"No! Your job is keeping him warm, isn't it? My job is making him food and feeding him."

Mina carried in a tray. "How're you feeling?"

"Awful."

"Think you're up for some dinner?"

Catching a whiff of her cooking made me painfully aware of my empty stomach. With her help, I sat up and opened my mouth. I let her feed me, as she asked; I didn't have the energy to say no.

"Do you remember collapsing out of nowhere?" Mina inquired. "You really gave me a scare."

"My bad."

"It's fine. You always do so much for me, Mr. Reiji. Now, it's my turn to care for you. Frankly, I'm glad to do it." Mina seemed genuinely happy.

COLDS AREN'T CAUGHT OUT OF NOWHERE

After I ate, she exclaimed, "Time for your medicine!" as if looking after a child. She handed me the same drugstore medication I'd given Ejil; I downed it in one gulp. The formula didn't actually have any effect on colds specifically. It enhanced your natural healing abilities, rather than striking the virus directly.

"Oh! Isn't this the first time you've treated yourself with your own medication?" Mina pointed out. "Those remedies are amazing, you know. Your cold will be gone in no time."

After bedtime, I slept like a rock. I woke up to yelling.

"Master no die!"

"No dying, Reiji!"

"Sir Reiji! Please awaken!"

Urgh...they're so loud.

It was apparently morning. Noela, Vivi, and Elaine—basically, all three of the young women I'd befriended—sat beside my bed. Vivi had a shift today; Elaine must've come by to hang out.

"Gosh, Noela!" Vivi gasped. "You scared me to death when you said Reiji wasn't waking up."

"Precisely!" Elaine exclaimed. She turned to me. "Thank goodness you're all right."

"Noela worried Master dead," the werewolf girl told me.

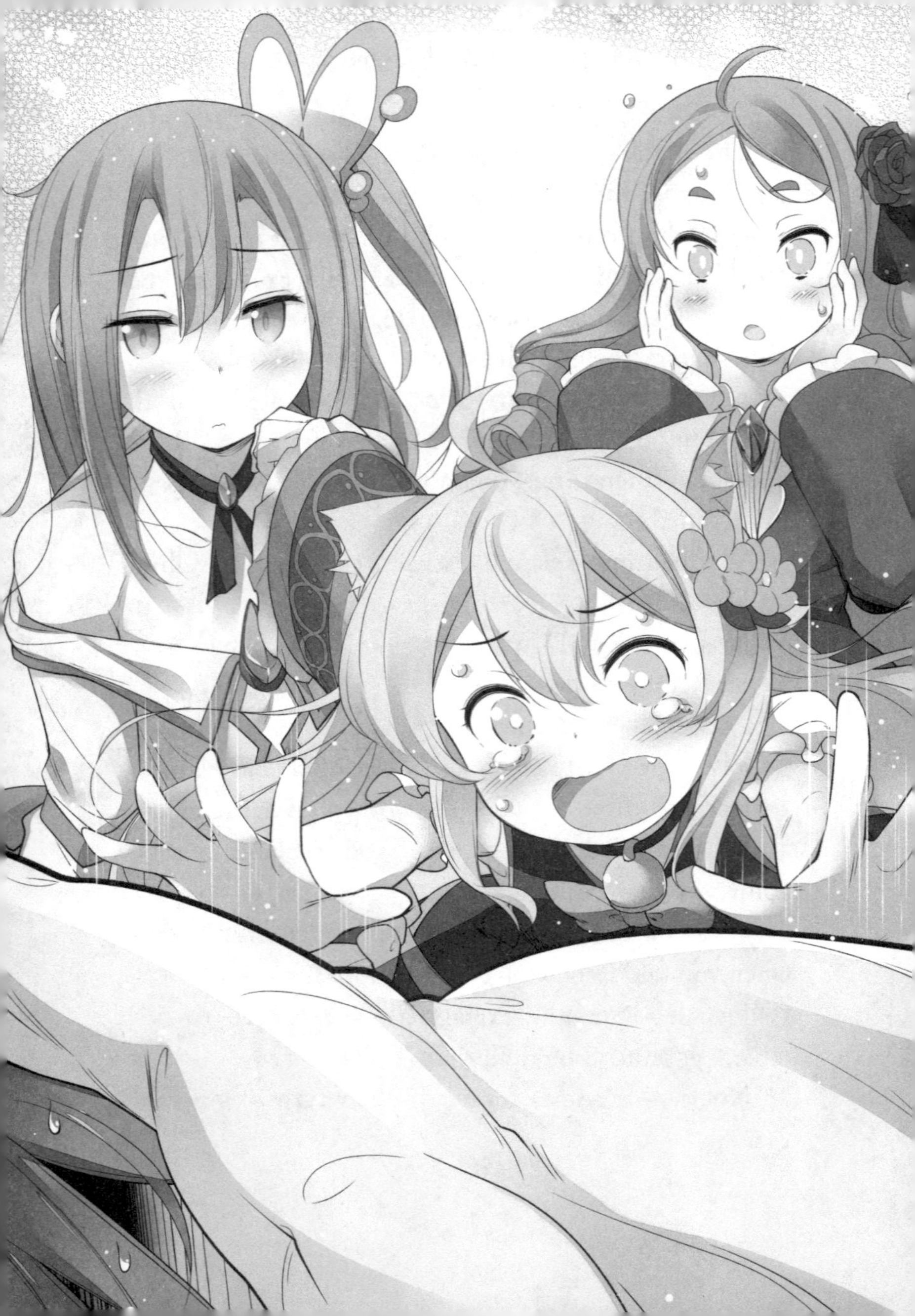

Elaine began feeding me what I assumed was Mina's cooking. "You don't want to catch my cold," I warned her.

Elaine smiled girlishly. "I'm not concerned, Sir Reiji! I'd like to look after you every now and then."

"Reiji! Reiji!" Vivi interjected. "Aren't you worried about me? I might catch a cold too, you know!"

"You get back to work." I knew I sounded like a jerk. Deep down, I was grateful to Vivi.

"Boo! You're playing favorites!" She touched my forehead to check my temperature; her hand was nice and cold. "I'm always chilly, so if you want me to cool you off, just let me know!"

"No good, Vivi," Noela objected. "Master cold. Bad! Mina say make warm."

"No, no. He's got a fever. He needs to cool down!"

"Vivi wrong!"

"I am not!"

"No yelling next to Sir Reiji!"

Before I could even appreciate having the girls around, I fell fast asleep. I woke up to more strange sounds, and my eyes spotted a bespectacled someone. The three young ladies were gone, replaced by Paula.

"Yo, Rei Rei. How you feeling?"

"Not great."

"I'm shocked. Guess even you can get sick, huh?" Paula laughed. "Mina's something else. Even her recovery food's stunningly tasty."

"Yeah...it is."

"C'mon, make your 'straight man' comeback! Where's the 'Don't eat my food, four-eyes'?!" Paula frowned, upset by the lack of repartee.

My bad. I don't recall ever calling you four-eyes, though.

"You better hurry up and get well," Paula continued. "You're the only one who plays along with me. I confuse Noela, and Mina just giggles. Oh!" She pulled out some cold medicine. "If you hit the sack, drink this. You didn't have the chance this morning, right? If it's too much for you to manage, I don't mind feeding it to you...mouth to mouth."

"I can handle it."

"Gosh, where'd your edge go? You really must be sick."

Paula watched, looking antsy, as I downed the medicine.

"Anna walked me to the drugstore," she added, handing me a fruit basket she'd placed at the foot of the bed. "She told me to give you this—the usual present for sick people! She should just have come by instead of being sheepish."

Anna...? She must mean Annabelle.

COLDS AREN'T CAUGHT OUT OF NOWHERE

"Get better soon!" Paula stroked my head gently before leaving.

The medicine kicked in, and I crashed again. I woke back up at night; my body was getting stiff from all this sleep. However, my head felt clear, and my fever had broken. My sluggishness was gone too. *I'm sure that's partly thanks to the meds, but it's also because everyone looked after me.*

Beside my bed, Mina and Noela were fast asleep. Either they were exhausted, or they'd gotten tired of monitoring me. I smiled and draped a nearby blanket over them.

Being sick really sucked, but sometimes, it was nice having others worry about you.

DRUGSTORE in AnotHer WORLD
~ The Slow Life of a Cheat Pharmacist ~

Bathtime Panic

ELAINE HAD STOPPED BY. As usual, after greeting us formally, she loitered at the counter.

"I'm having rather frightening nightmares lately," she noted with a serious expression. Her fingers twirled her drill-like curls.

"Hunh. Wow." That was the best response I could muster up. *How does she get ringlets like that? It's not like curlers exist in this world.*

As my mind drifted, Elaine glared. "Haven't you noticed how concerned I am, Sir Reiji? You've been acting quite cold toward me lately."

I sighed, exasperated. "Can you really blame me?" This was the fourth day in a row that Elaine had gone on about nightmares and insomnia. "So, in this recurring dream of yours, a giant Noela crushes you?"

"Mm-hmm. I had that same nightmare last night."

"You do realize the drugstore sells medicine and stuff, right?"

"I'm well aware, Sir Reiji. You tell me that every day."

"That's because you come here with the same issue every day." *Why's she treating me like I'm repetitive?*

"I'd like to spend the night," Elaine announced.

"Excuse me? No way. I'm guessing you didn't get your parents' permission. Since when are you such a delinquent?"

"I do have permission!" Elaine retorted, lifting her chin proudly. I could almost hear her victory cry. "Mother and Father even said I could stay as many nights as I wished. They trust you with me!"

Jeez. That's way too much trust! "Unfortunately for you, the head of this household—me—says no. Be good and go home, Drills."

"My father is lord of this region! In this town, what he says goes!"

"But this is my drugstore. I set the rules."

"Why must you be so stubborn?!" Elaine pouted.

"I don't see a problem with her staying a few days, Mr. Reiji." Mina poked her head into the store; she'd apparently been listening. "I'd enjoy the lively atmosphere."

Noela, of course, would also welcome Elaine. *I guess it's two to one.*

BATHTIME PANIC

I sighed loudly. "Fine. Just for one night, though. Even if you don't have a nightmare, you go home tomorrow."

"Thank you so much, Sir Reiji!" Elaine bounced like a rabbit. "Where's your room?"

"Over there. Er...why?"

"I decided to sleep in your bed!"

"Yeah, fat chance. You'll sleep with Mina and Noela," I declared, and Mina immediately backed me up.

"Sleeping with them definitely won't help me get past my nightmares," Elaine insisted.

"How would you know?"

"Well, sleeping in my parents' bed didn't help. But I'm sure *your* bed will work, since—um—I adore you so much, Sir Reiji!"

Mina groaned, covering her face with her hands.

Why's she getting flustered? "You're set on that?" I asked Elaine skeptically.

A person's mental state affected their dreams, so Elaine's nightmares might've been self-fulfilling prophecies. *She thinks she'll have nightmares, so when she sleeps, she actually does. On the other hand, if she believes her dreams will be fine, they'll be fine.*

Sleeping in the same bed as Mina or Ririka the elf might've flustered me. But Elaine was more or less Noela's age. No biggie. "One night only," I said with a sigh.

Elaine carried her suitcase to my room. *What is she, a traveling salesgirl?* Afterward, I got her to watch the drugstore with Noela.

People dreamed when they were just barely asleep, so I figured Elaine wouldn't have nightmares if she slept deeply and restfully. The fact that she said she'd feel comfortable in my bed was a safety net. *Let's see... Mina can brew her a relaxing herbal tea, and...*

It was time to whip up a new product. If I told Elaine it would help her sleep, I figured that would give her extra peace of mind. I closed myself up in the lab and followed my medicine-making skill's instructions, finishing just in time for dinner.

Mina popped in. "What's up?" I asked.

"Don't do anything weird with Elaine, Mr. Reiji."

"Who do you think I am?!" I'd planned to sleep on the sofa once Elaine nodded off. My shoulders slumped as I shook the bottle. "And...done."

TANGERINE BUBBLE BATH: Dissolves in hot water, producing suds that warm the body completely.

"What've you made, Mr. Reiji? It smells delightful."

"Uh, this is for bath time. It pretty much just makes

BATHTIME PANIC

you cozier." *If Elaine goes to bed while she's warm, she should sleep well enough not to have nightmares.*

Once Elaine and Noela closed the drugstore, the four of us ate together. Since Elaine was a new addition to the dinner table, the meal was rowdy and fun. Afterward, I filled the bathtub and let the three girls go first; I'd already explained to Mina how to use the bubble bath. Hearing them chatter in the bathroom, I called from the changing room to ask how they were doing.

"Smell good! Smell good!" Noela's voice called back.

"You'd better not drink the bubble bath, Noela!" I warned. "It only *smells* like oranges!"

"How you know?! Join, Master!"

"Nope."

"I'm putting the new product in the bathwater, Mr. Reiji!" Mina called. I could barely hear her over the sound of bubbles popping.

"O-oh, my word!" Elaine exclaimed. "Look at all the bubbles!"

I would've loved to head into the bathroom to check out the new product's results, but I was pretty sure the local mercs would get involved if I did. "Elaine, the bubble bath in the water prevents nightmares," I called. "Take a nice long bath."

"A-all right!"

"Smells good! Smells good!"

"No drinking the water!"

"How know? Master join!"

"I said that ain't happening."

I heard quiet splashes, and the voices of the three girls enjoying the bath. "Whew!"

"How is it, Mina?"

"Wonderful! The bubbles are so warm, and they're sticking to me! I feel like I'm going to heaven."

Since Mina was a ghost, that would've been bad. *Imagine if the girls finished their bath and she was gone. Talk about terrifying! Sorry, Mina, but no heaven right now.*

"It's as if the bubbles are dissolving everything bad!" Elaine exclaimed.

"Master! Master!"

"Noela, don't drink the water! There's a fresh potion chilling for you!"

"Garoo?! Then no drink!"

Thank god I keep a potion refrigerated just in case. "Take your time, ladies!" I called, heading into the living room.

My original plan had been to wait for the girls to finish bathing. *But, uh, they're not getting out...even though Noela's potion is nice and cold. And it's already been a half-hour.*

BATHTIME PANIC

Mina and Noela weren't the type to take long baths, which made me aware of a possibility. "Aw, crap. Don't tell me..."

I'd messed up. *I shouldn't have let those three bathe together! If they all doze off, who the heck's left to wake them?!*

That was when Paula's voice ran through my brain. *"This is what's called an accident! Falling asleep in the bathtub's pretty dangerous. You should go save them! No one's gonna blame you if you, uh, see something. Or touch something? It's all good, bro!"*

"All good, huh?" I muttered.

"What's all good, Rei Rei?"

"Gah!" I jumped back, spinning toward the voice.

Standing there was the *real* Paula. When she dropped in after the drugstore closed, it was usually for Mina's cooking. *Did she come here to eat dinner?*

Fortunately, that worked out for me. "Paula, I need to ask a tiny favor." I pulled the confused tool shop owner toward the bathroom, asking her to wake the girls.

Paula stood up straight and patted my head. "You're sure a gentleman, Rei Rei. I'm surprised!"

Whatever. Just get in there!

"If I were a dude," she continued, "I'd already have a massive nosebleed from fondling them while I woke 'em up!"

"Then it's a good thing you're *not* a dude." I opened the bathroom door and shoved Paula in, closing it quickly behind her.

"That wasn't very gentlemanly, Rei Rei!"

"I don't care. What's up in there?"

"Ack! Should've come in earlier."

"What do you mean?!"

"They're all unconscious!"

"The heat must've gotten to them. Pull them out!"

"Are you crazy, Rei Rei? Do you really think wimpy *me* can lift them?"

Kirio Reiji, it's time to man up.

Paula gave me directions as, eyes closed, I pulled all three women from the tub. "Why're you panicking, Rei Rei? You got this!"

"Shut up! You're just here for a free meal!"

Paula dressed the three, and I tucked them into their respective beds. I thought they'd wake up, but it never happened—not even for a second. After sleeping on the couch, I found the trio making breakfast.

"Ah! Good morning, Mr. Reiji," Mina said, beaming.

"Morning. Do you ladies remember fainting in the bathtub?"

The girls looked baffled. That made sense, considering that they'd been out cold.

BATHTIME PANIC

"I remember everything up to getting into the tub," Elaine replied. "After that, my memory's a blur till this morning."

Mina and Noela nodded.

"I bet. You three were dead to the world. Any nightmares, Elaine?"

Elaine's eyes widened in shock, and she gasped. "N-no! It's because I slept in your bed! I was much more comfortable there!"

"Nah. I think the bubble bath helped."

"I'll sleep over again to—"

"No need. I'll give you a bottle of bubble bath. Go home."

"See? You *are* cold toward me!"

"But a bubble bath's warm. Problem solved."

Elaine pouted again.

Afterward, I saw that the bubble bath bottle in the bathroom was empty; the girls had passed out in the tub because they used it all at once.

I wound up selling minuscule vials of bubble bath as a formula to help customers de-stress and get a good night's sleep. Locals were enthusiastic about the product, and it became popular as a treatment for a rough day.

104

10
Toughening Up

"LISTEN UP! You're all shit! Less than trash! Got it?!" Annabelle screeched.

Kirio Drugs' three female staff members sat in front of her like students in gym class. We were in a field just outside Kalta; I was watching nearby.

"Yes, Miss Annabelle!" my employees cried.

"What the hell do you mean, '*Miss Annabelle*'?! I ain't a teacher on a field trip! You've got two responses: 'Yes, ma'am!' and 'No, ma'am!' Got it?!"

Mina raised her hand. "Excuse me! Um, Annabelle, I don't think ladies should use words like 'shit.'"

I was pretty sure a vein popped in Annabelle's face. Even from a distance, I could tell she'd been irritated for a while.

"Don't talk back to your commanding officer!" She slapped the ground with the stick she carried. "Give me ten laps around the town walls! I'm gonna follow you losers, and if I catch up, I'm gonna kick your asses! Understand?!"

"Urgh! That'll hurt." Vivi slumped. "Why do you have to do that?"

Annabelle's stick smacked the ground again. "To make sure you maggots run properly!"

"Eek!"

Noela was unbothered by all this; she hadn't complained once. I guessed that this "training" seemed like nothing to her. She abruptly stood up and sprinted off.

"You!" Annabelle screamed. "Who told you to start running?!"

"Garroo?! You say run around town!" Noela yelled back.

"When I give the *order*, you run! Don't confuse things! Make sure you three run together!"

I'm not sure Noela's free spirit can stick to organized group tasks, I mused.

As for *why* Annabelle was drilling the ladies—Vivi had said yesterday that she wanted to get tougher. "Reiji, can you formulate a strengthening treatment for me?"

"You shouldn't ask for drugstore perks all the time," I'd replied. She'd requested the same thing a while back.

TOUGHENING UP

"Annabelle's tough—why not get her to train you? She's a professional mercenary. I bet she has awesome strategies."

Mina, who'd been listening, jumped in. "That sounds like a wonderful idea! I've been, um, concerned about a similar personal issue, so I'd like to participate as well. You know, just to tone up."

"Mina's in too?" I turned. "Hey, Noela, what about you?"

"Noela go! Noela protect Master! Wanna get stronger!"

They'd requested that Annabelle train them on our day off. Now my employees were running around Kalta's outskirts. Their terrifying, somewhat-demonic trainer chased after them, holding a stick.

"Good luck, ladies!" I cheered halfheartedly.

Mina waved with a big smile.

Vivi looked over; she seemed totally exhausted. "I'm doing my best, Reiji!"

Noela noticed me and dashed toward me.

"Hey! Don't disrupt things! Get *back* here!" Annabelle was screaming bloody murder.

Noela ignored her. She grabbed my arm, forcing me to jog. "Watching boring, Master! Run together!"

"Nah. I'm not interested in getting tougher! I just wanna chill and take a na—"

Noela dragged me up to Mina and Vivi.

"Yay! You're running with us?"

"Let's give it our all, Reiji!"

Their warm welcomes made it harder to stop jogging.

"You're slowing us down!" Annabelle roared at me.

"I-I'm sorry!" I panted.

And so, I wound up running too. To make matters worse, we were going pretty fast. My stamina soon hit rock bottom, but anytime I slowed down, Annabelle whacked my butt. *Smack!*

"Ow!"

"Huh? My men love it when I do that!"

Don't lump me in with those perverts! I thought indignantly. *I just want to go home. I should've hung out with Zeral, not come to watch! Remind me who recommended Annabelle coach the girls?* Breathless, I completed ten laps around Kalta. *I feel like my HP hit zero ages ago!*

"Stand up!" Annabelle barked. "Give me a thousand push-ups, sit-ups, and back extensions!"

Impossible! I tried to leave, crawling on the ground like a bug.

Someone grabbed my ankles. "Where're you going, Reiji? Didn't you promise to get stronger with me?"

"When?! I'm not some Saiy*n stoically pursuing strength!"

Annabelle smacked the ground. "Hey, Maggot V! Stop slacking!"

I guess Maggot V is Vivi—so Mina is M, Noela is N, and I'm R.

"Eek! She's so scary," Vivi wailed. "I stopped because Reiji tried to desert, Captain!"

She snitched on me!

Annabelle came over, glaring daggers. "Maggot R, who gave you permission to run from the battlefield?!"

"It was a tactical retreat, ma'am!"

"*You* don't make that call!"

My shoulders scrunched in fear as Annabelle's stick swung down, striking my thighs. *Thunk!*

Huh? It didn't hurt. She must've gone super easy on me. What a good woman!

"I was leaving to develop a treatment to maximize muscle gain, ma'am!" I declared.

"Hunh! You can do that?"

"Yes, ma'am!"

"Fine! Maggot R, head to your lab and get to work!"

Thank goodness. I found an escape!

"Is it just me," Mina interjected, "or is Annabelle extra soft on Mr. Reiji?"

"Noela think so."

"I don't think commanding officers should play

favorites like that," Mina continued. "Bringing personal feelings into the mix disrupts squad discipline and leads to infighting. What do you think, ma'am?"

"Shut up! No one gave you permission to weigh in!"

"Don't think you can control everything by pulling rank!" Mina snapped. "If you're giving orders based on your feelings for Reiji, I can't help wondering whether you're qualified to lead the Red Cat Brigade!"

Annabelle fell silent, unable to respond.

"Hey, Mina," I intervened. "Annabelle took time out of her day to coach you guys. Stop messing with her."

"All right!" Mina replied cheerfully.

"Maggot M! Five hundred extra push-ups, sit-ups, and extensions for you!"

"Aw," Mina muttered, but started the exercises nevertheless.

"I'm gonna go whip up a treatment. Hang in there!" I told her.

I guess that's the regime Annabelle puts the Red Cat Brigade through, I mused as I headed back to town. The brigade's job was to protect Kalta and fight off invaders, so it made sense that the mercenaries had to train hard. Still, I couldn't help admiring them for doing that kind of workout day after day. If I developed a way to build strength easily and effectively, though,

TOUGHENING UP

the brigade wouldn't need a super-long daily training regime.

Back at the drugstore's lab, I mixed together a ton of ingredients and—using my energy potion as the base—successfully developed a new potion formula.

> **POWER POTION:** Improves muscle recovery. Enhances muscle gain. Drink after exercise.

"Now it should be easier to build muscle without working out for hours," I murmured, sipping the vanilla-flavored potion. It went down quite nicely.

After making several power potions, I headed back to the field. Vivi lay on the ground like a corpse. Mina panted, her hair tousled. I could tell just by looking at them how tough Annabelle's boot camp had been. *Thank goodness I left when I did.* Noela was the only one who seemed unaffected. *I suppose that's to be expected of a werewolf.*

"Master back!" she cried.

"Finished training, Noela?"

She wagged her tail. "Easy-peasy!"

"Hey, Maggot N," Annabelle broke in. "What do you say to joining the brigade?"

Annabelle, I understand attempting to recruit Noela, but she's a free spirit. I doubt she could handle merc life.

"Nope. Noela like time with Master."

I stroked Noela's head thankfully. *What can I say? I adore her too.*

"Oh—before I forget, I made these." I handed power potions to Noela and Annabelle, explaining their effects.

Annabelle scrutinized the bottle. "Hrm. You're saying this'll make building muscle easier?"

"Someone who's already ripped won't see super-obvious results," I replied. "But strength-training newbies will spot changes easily. With this stuff, your usual regime will give them way more results."

Noela uncapped the bottle, taking a sniff and a sip. "Sweet! Get buff!" She clenched her fists tightly.

I couldn't help laughing. "You won't build muscle that easily."

"Hrm." Noela focused. Suddenly, her arms bulked up before my very eyes. I did a double take; the werewolf girl now had massive tan biceps.

"Wha—?! It works *that* quickly?!" Annabelle and I shrieked, stunned. We watched Noela's tan, muscular arms rub her cheeks lovingly.

"Wh-what's wrong, Noela?"

"Noela hear biceps talk, Master." Even her voice was deeper now.

TOUGHENING UP

"No freaking way!" I gasped. "World-class bodybuilders say stuff like that!"

"Hear them! 'Exercise me more! Make stronger!'"

Who is this strange girl? Where's her usual cuteness? I prefer the sweet, fluffy Noela to this bulked-up beast! She's even kissing her biceps! "Come back to us, Noela!" I wailed. "Come back to me!"

"What happened to Noela?" Mina asked in a deep voice.

I turned. "Uh, my new potion worked a little too well. Noela apparently hears her biceps talking."

Wait. Is it just me, or is Mina's voice kind of husky?

Before I had time to consider that, I saw that Mina—who once looked gentle—now had a tan six-pack, a tank top, and shorts. She flexed her core with a macho grunt; at her feet was an empty potion bottle.

"*You* drank it too?!"

"Why, yes! I was parched, so I enjoyed your refreshments."

The potion had had almost no effect on me—but I'd only taken a sip, and I'd barely done any strength training.

"Tee hee! How silly of Noela, saying she hears her biceps. What's gotten into her?" Mina caressed her abdomen lovingly, like an expectant mother. However, she had the opposite of a rounded navel; her fingers rubbed her sculpted muscles. "That said, I *can* hear my abs talking to me."

"'What's gotten into her?!' What's gotten into *you*?! You're imagining you can *hear* your muscles talking? Have you flipped?!"

"I'm entranced by these perfectly toned abs," Mina continued. "Lord Six-Pack is saying, 'You've worked hard for that beautiful body, and those abs are proof! Show them off to the world! Gah ha ha ha!'"

"Who the hell is *Lord Six-Pack*?!"

"Wonderful," Mina sighed, continuing to whisper to herself.

Who is this woman?! Where's my adorable Mina? I loved her kind smile! "Come back to us, Mina!" I wailed. "Come back to me!"

Mina's eyes met Noela's, and the girls exchanged a powerful handshake. They began praising each other's defined muscles, then discussed their workout routines passionately.

There's no room for me here. I don't belong. As for Vivi, she was still dead to the world. *I should leave her alone too.*

I headed back to the dazed Annabelle and handed her several power potions, cautiously suggesting that she dilute them to weaken their effects.

Mina and Noela's muscle high lasted about an hour. After they returned to normal, we headed back to town; I carried Vivi piggyback.

"Reiji, I bet the voices they heard were muscle spirits!" Vivi told me.

"Think so?" I asked. I honestly didn't care anymore.

Mina and Noela held my arms. "You don't need to get ripped," I assured them. "After all, we run a pharmacy."

"If you say so, Mr. Reiji."

"Noela agree!"

The four of us exchanged smiles. Today, my life in a world without bloodshed, battle, or permanently ginormous muscles had been as fun as ever.

DRUGSTORE IN ANOTHER WORLD
~ The Slow Life of a Cheat Pharmacist ~

Kirio Reiji's Studying Meds

AROUND LUNCHTIME, Mina remembered something she'd meant to bring up. "Is it just me, or has Paula stopped coming by?"

"Hunh. You're right."

It had actually been ten days since we last saw the tool shop owner. It usually wouldn't have been a big deal for a customer not to visit for a week or two. However, Paula had constantly dropped in to eat or hang out. She'd shown up at Kirio Drugs at least every other day—no exaggeration.

I turned to Noela, who was gulping down her lunch. "Noela, do you know why?" She only raised her head to shake it, then went back to pigging out.

"Correct me if I'm wrong, but Paula lives alone at the tool shop, doesn't she?" Mina asked.

"That's right."

"I'm worried."

Paula's ten-day absence really was concerning, since she was a young woman living alone. It would've been weird if we were unconcerned about whether she was injured or sick.

"I'll swing by her place after lunch," I assured Mina.

"Please do. I hope everything's fine."

Same here.

I headed to the tool shop right after we'd eaten. Things outside looked okay. The store itself seemed to be operating; the "open" sign was up.

"You in, Paula?" I called, entering. Paula was at the counter, but rather than sleeping as usual, she was writing with a fountain pen. "You *are* here. Man, can't you answer a guy?"

"What's the big deal, Rei Rei? Unlike you, I'm pretty busy."

Wow. Just because she has stuff to take care of, she's treating me like a lazy bum? The tables were usually turned, so I couldn't help feeling annoyed. "Sorry. I'm just here to check on you."

Paula didn't even look at me. She glanced at a folder to her right, then jotted more notes on the paper in front of her.

What's she doing? "Don't tell me you're studying," I said skeptically. *Paula, of all people?*

"Then I guess I won't tell you!"

"What're you studying for, exactly?"

"My license renewal exam comes up every two years."

I wondered what "license" she meant. Before I could ask, Paula pointed at a large parchment sheet on the wall behind her; it seemed to be a formal document. Paula's name was on it, and it apparently confirmed that she had the right to appraise objects.

I don't remember seeing this certificate. I must never have noticed it.

"Any tool or equipment shop with this license is a formally recognized appraiser," Paula informed me. "That basically means they're not ripping customers off or buying stuff cheap."

"That explains the studying." She was making sure her license renewal went smoothly.

"There are idiots who buy and sell licenses," Paula added, "but their stores typically fail in no time. Trust's the most important thing in this business. Especially to me."

She pushed up her glasses. Since she was studying, she came off as oddly intellectual for once.

"Argh! I'm so done with all this!" Paula exclaimed.

She turned to me. "Whoa—you're here, Rei Rei? Why didn't you say something?"

"Was our entire conversation just a hallucination?"

She leaned over the counter, grabbing my arm. "Can you do me a little favor?" she practically purred at me. "Make a treatment that'll keep me from slipping on my test!"

I doubted she meant "slipping" in the physical sense—but now wasn't the time to match wits.

"If I fail, I'll have to close down," she added. "People trust licensed stores so much, a license is vital for tool shop owners!"

"Remember, formulating new treatments takes a while," I said. "I can't guarantee I'll finish one by the time you need it. When's your exam?"

"Tomorrow. Tee hee!"

I gaped.

"This is bad, Rei Rei!" Paula wailed. "I have to score at least 85 percent, or I'm doomed! And I just scored 20 on the practice test! Sorry, I lied—I scored *ten*!"

"Doesn't make much difference. What the hell have you been doing up until now?"

"Studying. Duh."

"With *those* scores?"

Paula pouted. "You're a meanie, Rei Rei!"

KIRIO REIJI'S STUDYING MEDS

"Where's the exam held?"

"In the next town over, so I've gotta leave early in the morning to make it. I'm doing my best, but the test covers *so* much!"

Am I supposed to prescribe a product to keep her from failing?

"Wait. I might be able to make you something!" My medicine-making skill was reacting, after all. "You'll still have to study, though."

"Whoa! You thought up a prescription?"

"Listen, Paula. This'll be a race against time, so I'll go make your treatment and come back."

"I love you, Rei Rei!"

"Stop messing around. Just stay here and study." I dashed out of the tool shop and headed home breathlessly.

Noela was keeping an eye on the drugstore. "Why hurry?" she asked.

"Just some work! I need your help in the lab, Noela."

"Got it!"

She came back to the lab with me. By this point, Noela was practically the perfect medicine-making assistant; thanks to that, I finished the product much earlier than I expected.

I decided it'd be quickest to send the lightning-fast Noela to deliver Paula's prescription to the tool shop.

In her little backpack, I put ten energy potions, plus the new medicine I'd just made. I also included a piece of paper with directions and a warning.

"All ready!" Noela cried.

"Noela, launch!"

"Arrrooooo!"

Noela sprinted out of the lab at top speed, and I followed. She adopted her wolf form as she exited the house on all fours, kicking up a dust trail behind her. Some bystanders let out surprised cries, but since this was an emergency, all I could do was hope they forgave her this once. *Anyway, she'll come home in her normal form.*

I'd now done everything I could; all that was left was for Paula to give the licensing test all she had. The treatment I'd made would support her studying.

After some time passed, Noela—in her humanoid form—trotted back into the drugstore. The backpack she wore made her look like a schoolkid coming home from a field trip.

"How's Paula?" I asked.

"Serious. Say thanks to Master."

I felt it was a wee bit early for gratitude. *But, hey, I'll take it anyhow.*

◆◆◆

The next day, I was too worried to get anything done. Had Paula slept okay? Woken up on time? Made it to the exam venue? Yikes—what if she forgot her registration form? *Wait...I don't even know whether this world* has *those.* At any rate, I was distracted for the entire day.

◆◆◆

Three days later, Paula finally popped into the drugstore.

"Look at this!" she shrieked as she saw me, showing me her brand-new license.

"Whoa, awesome! Congrats. Glad things worked out."

"It was all thanks to your prescription, Rei Rei," Paula declared. "That stuff was seriously crazy! I'll count on you next time!"

"You're the one who made the effort. You read the instructions, right?"

"Ah...maybe you're right! I guess I tried pretty hard. Tee hee!"

"Don't get a big head." I flicked Paula's forehead, and she giggled.

Paula's request for a treatment to keep her from failing had been vague, but basically, she'd needed something to help her study.

Why do people memorize stuff over and over when they're studying? I'd thought. *Because they forget.* If you eliminated the "forgetting" part of hitting the books, you'd learn way more effectively. You'd see the light at the end of the tunnel after minimal studying.

With that in mind, I'd formulated Paula's prescription.

> **ACED-T:** Locks in short-term memory.

Personally, I thought the aced-T was kind of amazing. Still, it was ultimately a support item, since it required you to memorize whatever you were studying. Thus, Paula's exam score came down to how much information she could stuff into her head.

"I seriously didn't sleep at all," she laughed. "Major cramming."

That got a smirk out of me; I could totally picture her studying all night.

Tip tap! Tip tap! Paula skipped up to me.

"You seriously saved me this time," she said, kissing my cheek.

"Thanks again!" she giggled, waving before she left.

She totally just kissed me, right? I touched my cheek absentmindedly but soon felt a gaze coming at me from behind. I turned around.

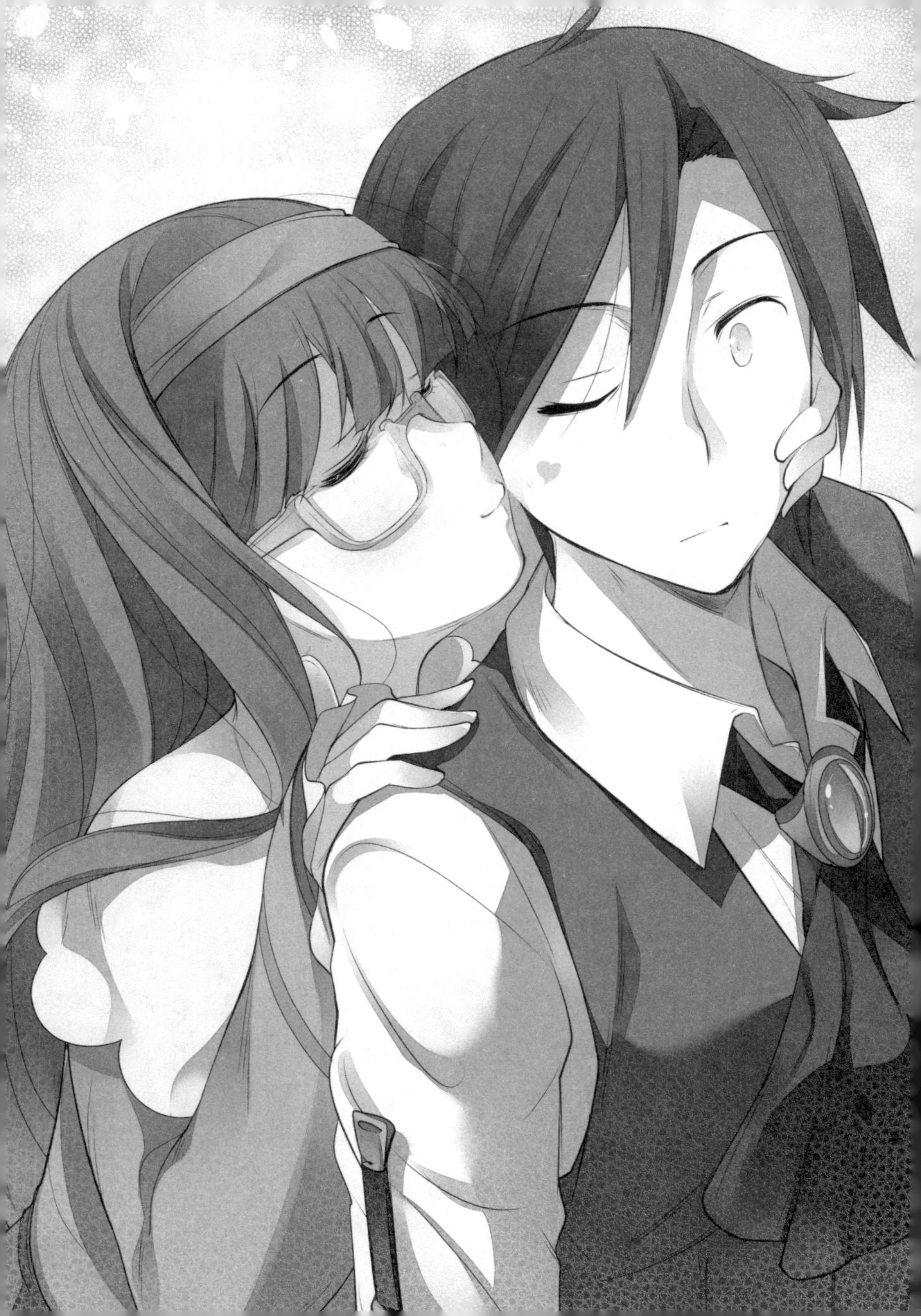

Mina looked...unhappy. "I suppose you're going without dinner today!"

"Wait! Why?!"

"That's how the cookie crumbles!" She turned and left.

"What the heck did I do?" I sighed. *How will I get her out of that bad mood? I'll have to splurge on some pricey sweets.*

I spent some time mulling over how to make up with Mina.

Bad at Drinking Parties

I WAS WATCHING THE STORE when someone whispered, "Sir Medicine God!"

Confused, I looked around and spotted Doz—the Red Cat Brigade's vice captain—by the drugstore entrance. He looked around nervously, his massive frame hunched over.

"What's up, buddy?" I called. "Is Annabelle with you?"

"The boss ain't here."

That's odd. Wonder what happened. Doz usually dropped in with Annabelle.

The vice captain came toward the counter quietly and sat across from me. "Save me, Medicine God."

"Oh, boy. This sounds bad."

"No kidding. This time every year, the Red Cat Brigade rents the Rabbit Tavern for our annual party."

Hunh. They have an annual party?

Actually, I remembered the Rabbit Tavern's barmaid Rena telling me, "It's party season, so we're awfully busy! But, hey, busy periods aren't bad!" At the time, I'd been surprised that the tavern had a "party season." Apparently, one event was the Red Cat Brigade's celebration.

"Wait," I told Doz. "Why do you need my help with that? Won't you guys just have a blast eating great food and getting drunk?"

"Well, Medicine God, the boss ain't a drinker. And I'm a total lightweight. Everybody else gets loaded, though."

"You're not great with drinking parties, huh? I totally get it. I've never been big on them." For a moment, I felt like I'd found a comrade.

However, Doz shook his head. "Really, it's just...if everyone else gets smashed, and I barely finish my drink, how's that gonna look to the boss?"

He seems nervous about explaining this in detail. Why is he concerned about Annabelle's reaction, but not the others'? Ah...I get it. "You want to impress Annabelle."

"That's not..." Doz scratched his head shyly. "Well, yeah, basically."

I understood why he wanted to look cool in front of her; Annabelle was stunning. "What'd you do last year?"

BAD AT DRINKING PARTIES

"I blacked out after a few mugs of beer. The next morning, I woke up in a barrel with the worst hangover. The boss laughed her butt off. This year, I wanna walk her home like a gentleman."

As a man, and as the Red Cat Brigade's vice captain, he wanted to overwrite last year's party at any cost. *Hunh.*

"That's why I need your help, Medicine God."

"Gotcha," I replied. "I totally understand how you feel, Doz. I'm a man too, you know?"

"Could you make a product that turns booze into water?"

"I'll whip something up for you."

Doz's large, muscular hand clasped mine and shook it as he thanked me over and over. I understood now why he'd visited so furtively; he didn't want Annabelle or the mercenaries to figure out what he was doing.

I had the vice captain wait while I headed to the lab. Regardless of whether Annabelle was his boss, there was only one reason a man would want to look good in front of a woman. That was why I wanted to help. I gathered the herbs I'd use off the shelves. *A work party, huh? Maybe the drugstore should hold one too.*

The lab door opened, and Mina and Noela entered. A sweet smell came from the kitchen.

"Made cookies, Master! Eat!" Noela presented me with a single star-shaped cookie.

I took the cookie with my teeth; it was so warm and crunchy, fresh out of the oven. "This is great!"

"Garroo!" Noela's tail wagged at maximum speed. *Swoosh!*

Mina had brought a basket of cookies too. "We just baked these," she told me. "I'll leave them here, so help yourself, all right? Oh—would you like tea?"

"I'll have some later, thanks."

Noticing that I'd dirtied my hands preparing the herbs, Noela fed me another cookie.

As I kept working, I asked, "Hey, what do you two say to a get-together with the other drugstore employees?"

Mina tapped her chin. "If you'd like to do that, Mr. Reiji, we should! Now that Ejil and Vivi work here, I'd love to have a welcome event."

Mina, Noela, and I did take a trip before. It might be nice to find time for all five of us to go somewhere.

"Noela want Vivi welcome party!" the werewolf girl exclaimed.

"What about Ejil?"

"Ejil whatever," she answered immediately.

She really hates you, Ejil.

"C'mon, don't say that," I replied with a strained smile, then finished preparing the herbs. "All right, this should do it."

BAD AT DRINKING PARTIES

> **LIVER ALLY X:** Accelerates liver functions, breaking alcohol down more quickly. Prevents hangovers/vomiting due to intoxication.

I handed Doz the finished formula and explained its effects, directing him to take Liver Ally X before eating.

◆Another Side◆

Doz did as Medicine God Reiji said, gulping down the new treatment concocted to help him stomach alcohol. He made sure to get rid of the empty bottle so that nobody at the party would find out what he'd gotten from the drugstore.

He was honestly skeptical of the Liver Ally X, but the medicine god had yet to steer him wrong. Doz figured there was no way Reiji would mess up.

"This doesn't turn alcohol into water, got it?" Reiji had warned him, explaining that the Liver Ally X would just increase his alcohol tolerance.

After swallowing the treatment, Doz stood in front of the Rabbit Tavern. The other mercenaries were already inside, making toasts back and forth. He slapped both his cheeks gently.

"What the heck are you doin' there?"

"Whoa!" Doz jumped and turned around to see Annabelle standing nearby. She was wearing her hair down instead of in her usual ponytail; it was sexy, in a way. "B-Boss, I didn't see you there."

"I can't go inside while you're in the way. Get your big ass in there!" She kicked Doz in the butt, causing him to groan.

The mercenaries cheered as Doz and Annabelle entered the tavern. Everyone had a wooden mug in hand, and the tables were already laden with tons of food.

"This is for you, Boss!" Rena, the Rabbit Tavern's barmaid, handed Annabelle a mug of juice. She was used to the Red Cat Brigade's yearly ritual. Doz also got a mug, but his was full of foamy ale.

"You all got your booze?" Annabelle called. "No need for dumb opening speeches, is there?"

"Who wants that junk?!" the mercenaries called.

"Damn straight. Cheers!"

"Cheers!" The entire brigade chugged their first drink, clearing their throats in tandem.

"Huh? I'm not feeling anything." Doz put down his mug. He'd drained it, but the usual light blow to his brain didn't come. "You're seriously amazing, Medicine God!"

Each table Annabelle visited exploded with excitement. Not only was she a fantastic mercenary, but she really bloomed on the battlefield. More importantly, she truly cared for her men.

Annabelle approached Doz—who was posing victoriously—with a strange expression. "Is something up with you tonight?"

"I'm a brand-new man, Boss!"

"Well, ain't you talking tough?"

They gently bumped their mugs together and gulped their second drinks. This year, the beer didn't make Doz feel awful at all. "Rena, hon, get me another mug!"

"Er...are you sure?" Rena hesitated. "At the last party..."

Annabelle grinned and pointed at Doz. "Grab this oaf somethin' to drink for my sake, Rena. He claims he's a brand-new man!"

"Sure thing!" Rena replied, heading to the kitchen.

Doz made his way to the other tables, enjoying his fellow mercs' company as he bumped his third mug against theirs. Drinks, conversation, food, more drinks, more stupid conversation—this was the first time he'd truly enjoyed one of these parties.

But what about Annabelle? Ain't it lonely to be the only one sober?

Doz spotted the Red Cat Brigade's captain leaving the tavern and trailed her.

"What're you doin' following me?" Annabelle barked. "Go enjoy the celebration."

"I'm your second-in-command. This is where I belong, Boss."

"That so?" Annabelle sat on the grass. Doz sat next to her. "Y'know," she mused, "it's a big deal that a merc brigade working outta a tiny town made it another year healthy and happy."

"We've got your charm to thank for that, Boss! If I were in charge, things'd never be like this." When they'd started out, Doz remembered, it was just him and Annabelle.

"The hell you talkin' about? We got that motley crew this far half 'cause of you!"

Annabelle looked away. Her moonlit profile seemed all the more sophisticated, and her cheeks were pink. Doz knew that wasn't just from the tavern's heat and excitement. He was different tonight, and something in his heart exploded.

"Boss...!"

"Hmm?"

Grasping Annabelle's shoulders, he puckered his lips.

"What're you doin', you dumbass?!" Annabelle yelped. "That's gross!"

He passed out from agony as she kicked him square in the groin, then punched him four or five times in the face. Doz's last memory that night was the sound of bones breaking.

◆Reiji's Side◆

"So, this year, you literally got knocked unconscious?"

"Er...yeah."

"Dude, what's wrong with you?!" I couldn't help sighing loudly. "You had a good atmosphere going, and you just...ruined it!"

Doz had dropped in to discreetly tell me how the work party went. The broad-shouldered mercenary had massive, panda-like black eyes, and both cheeks had clearly taken several blows.

"Nah," he insisted. "This year, I got to see the boss's bashful expression. That alone was good enough for me!"

"You're satisfied with that?! Stop being softhearted, old man!" I'd honestly been wrapped up in his puppy-love tale until halfway through.

"Reiji—no, Medicine God—it's all thanks to that Liver Ally X that I had fun. Thanks so much!"

"Well, I'm glad I could help." *Guess Doz feels like it worked.* "Fun is what it's all about."

"Plus, I deepened my bond with the boss," the vice captain added. He excused himself with a friendly grin, marching his massive body out of the drugstore.

"You sure you didn't 'deepen' the hole you're digging yourself into?" I mumbled.

I found it fascinating to watch his relationship with Annabelle progress, and I decided to support him as much as I could if he needed help again. *I just can't leave that dumb vice captain hanging.*

13
That Seasonal Stuff

VIVI, NOELA, MINA, AND I were working in the drugstore.

"Achoo!" Vivi sneezed, then sniffled loudly.

As if the lake spirit had infected her, Noela did the same thing. "Achee!"

"AAAH-CHOOOOO!" Mina sneezed like an old man. Everyone gawked at her. "Um, forget you heard that. *Achoo!* That was the real one."

Yeah, right. Her panic betrayed her embarrassment.

Everyone was sniffling and sneezing an awful lot recently. Ejil had been doing the same thing yesterday. "The humans are using that cowardly bioweapon again, Doctor," he'd grumbled.

I kept an eye on everybody's symptoms, but it didn't seem like a cold was going around. After all, I was perfectly fine, and I lived and worked with these four. "What's wrong, ladies?"

Noela rubbed her eyes. "Want eye drops, Master. Make eyes feel better."

"I'd like some as well, Reiji," said Mina.

"Me too!" Vivi exclaimed. "Honestly, my eyes are just so itchy!"

"Hrm..." I paused. "Eye drops are selling out lately. Are the townspeople having the same issues?"

"Almost everyone's eyes get itchy this time of year," Vivi said.

Based on their symptoms, are they dealing with allergies?

"Are you girls allergic to pollen?" That was hard to believe, since Vivi and Noela weren't human.

"Allergic to pollen?" they repeated, looking confused.

I guess they've never heard those words together. "The wind can carry plant pollen, which causes allergy symptoms. Runny noses, itchy eyes, that kind of thing."

I'd never had pollen allergies, but they must be rough; some people actually had them treated at a hospital. "I wonder whether cedar trees exist here," I muttered.

The girls took me seriously. "I don't know what cedar is, but I might know where this 'pollen allergy' comes from," Vivi declared. "In the woods, there's a huge tree that blossoms this time of year. People with runny noses and itchy eyes can't even get close to it. Do you think that's the root of our problem?"

If a nature spirit like Vivi thinks so, it must *be that tree.* I considered leaving it alone; I'd make money selling eye drops, and I was pretty much unaffected by the pollen personally. On the other hand, the truth was that the townspeople—and my employees—were suffering. I couldn't just do nothing.

"I should probably go inspect this tree," I concluded. "If we don't have an exact grasp on what causes this, it'll be impossible to create a treatment. Noela, Vivi, care to come with me?"

They shook their heads.

"Pollen allergy scary," Noela moaned.

"You *already* have a pollen allergy."

"If you're allergic to pollen, you can't get near that tree," Vivi reminded me.

"Can't you at least show me the way?"

They sneezed simultaneously. *Guess that's their answer.*

"I'll make you lunch!" Mina announced, fleeing into the kitchen.

These three are really throwing me under the bus. It's sad. "Guess I've got no choice."

Deciding to head off alone, I packed repellent to keep monsters away. I also put some Translator DX into my bag so I could communicate with animals if necessary. I grabbed my lunch from Mina, and Vivi drew me a map; then I proceeded on my journey.

It'd been quite some time since I'd followed the road outside Kalta solo. Eventually, I found the entrance to the woods where we gathered herbs and materials. I checked the map Vivi had given me, but only a moment passed before I folded it back up.

"This is completely unreadable." *It's full of nonsensical scribbles. She really thought I'd understand this? Good work, Vivi.*

"Well, if it isn't Reiji baby."

"Ah, Reiji!"

The elf siblings Ririka and Kururu had appeared before me in my hour of need.

"Hey," I said. "You two going somewhere together?"

"We're actually walking to your place," Kururu replied. "We just ran out of potions."

"What about you? Heading into the woods all alone?" asked Ririka.

Frankly, seeing those two together reminded me of how insanely attractive they both were. A human could never hope to acquire that degree of beauty; the elves were almost too stunning to look at directly. Anyway, I explained the issue with the big tree that Vivi had described, adding that I'd guessed that its pollen was causing allergic reactions in Kalta.

"You must mean the Zeg Tree," replied Ririka.

"I bet that's the one," Kururu agreed.

"Awesome. Hey, if it's not too much hassle, could you tell me how to get there?" With a pained smile, I showed them Vivi's map.

Kururu cleared his throat theatrically. "I'd be happy to guide you, young man!"

"Uh, that's fine. I'm not asking *you* to," I quickly interrupted, glancing at Ririka.

"Huh?" she gasped. "Y-you mean *I* should guide you?!"

"Ririka, my dearest sister," Kururu snapped, "this is the perfect time to read the room and give me some alone time with Reiji."

"Alone time...?" Ririka touched her hair, glancing up at me before averting her eyes.

"I brought monster repellent, but I'd rather not head into the woods alone," I told her. "If I got lost, it'd be bad."

Kururu tried to whisper something to her from behind. "My dear sis—OOF!" Ririka's elbow delivered what looked like a critical hit to her brother's solar plexus. He collapsed, stunned.

"I-I'd be happy to guide you, Reiji," Ririka offered.

"Thanks a lot."

Kururu struggled to his feet and tossed his hair. "I'm worried about you two going alone. I'll have to join you."

"No need," Ririka said. "I can guide Reiji just fine."

"If I don't protect Reiji baby, who will?"

How dare he say that with a straight face?! "You're the only one chasing me, Kururu."

"You go buy the potions, brother."

"Oh, Ririka—I forgot that I *also* have to run an errand at the Zeg Tree. Ha ha ha!"

Ririka and I sighed simultaneously. *Guess he's hell-bent on coming with us.*

The younger elf had me follow her; behind us strolled Kururu. Before long, I told him to walk ahead of me. Having him back there made me nervous.

Thanks to the drugstore repellent, our little party made its way through the woods without much trouble.

"What's the deal with this Zeg Tree?" I asked.

Kururu was the one to answer. "Our tribe worships it. It actually belongs to a common tree species used for lumber. This particular tree is enormous, though, and produces tons of pollen."

"All the foresters working in the woods know it's sacred, so no one tries to chop it down," Ririka added. "Look! that's it."

She pointed ahead, toward a tree that was indeed gigantic. It had evidently been there for decades—no, centuries. It stood so tall, it would've been fair to call it a symbol of the forest itself.

"Whoa!" *That tree's so majestic, I feel like I'm seeing some international landmark. Its trunk's so frigging thick, one person could never fell that thing—it'd take dozens to even encircle it. I can't believe a tree like this was in the forest all along. Hrm? Wait... My nose is starting to bug me.*

I wasn't allergic to pollen, so if even *I* felt sniffly, I couldn't imagine someone with actual allergies trying to get this close. It would've been impossible. "Are your noses clear?" I asked the elves.

"Mine's perfectly fine."

"Same, Reiji baby. We elves are born and raised in the woods, unlike humans. We may be immune to all sorts of things," Kururu added. "I'd never even considered that pollen could bother you."

Ririka nodded.

I looked up at the Zeg Tree, and my jaw dropped. "Man, this thing's huge."

At first, I'd figured that we could just chop it down if it caused too many issues. But according to the elf siblings, the Zeg Tree was an object of worship, which ruled that out. Plus, felling a tree that astounding would feel wrong.

I doubted that the Zeg Tree was the sole cause of Kalta's pollen issue. *Still, if we do something about it, I bet we'll at least halve the number of allergy patients. The problem with minimizing the pollen is that it's a natural part of a tree's life cycle.*

I sat on one of the tree's large roots and started eating the sandwiches Mina had given me.

Ririka glanced at them. "Did, um, Mina make those?"

"Yeah. Want one?"

"No, that's quite all right. She made them for you, after all."

Kururu cleared his throat. "Reiji baby, would you like a peach for dessert?"

"Please tell me you mean a *literal* peach."

"Huh? O-of course." Kururu not-so-subtly removed his hands from his waistband, clasping them behind his back.

Ririka gave her brother a look of pure disdain. "You're making a fool of yourself."

I agreed. "That line was terrible. You're not a grade-schooler. It's pointless to humor your 'shameless flirt' schtick if you can't come up with something more unique."

"Could you stop giving feedback?!"

As we finished lunch, I noticed something. There was

no wind, but the Zeg Tree kept spitting out enormous clouds of pollen. *Pwoosh!* More pollen erupted; sometimes it thinned, but sometimes the tree produced cloud after cloud.

When I really focused on the great tree, I could see eyes, a nose, and a mouth. *Hm...maybe I can talk to this thing.* Reaching into my bag, I sipped the Translator DX. Not expecting much, I approached the Zeg Tree. "Um, hi. Can you hear me?"

"A child of man is talking to me...?"

Woo-hoo! It worked! "My name's Kirio Reiji," I said. "Um, your pollen's giving townspeople runny noses and making them sneeze. I came here today hoping we could figure out a solution."

"I'm incapable of controlling the pollen you speak of," the Zeg Tree replied. "It exists so that I can spread my seed as...as a...ACHOO!" A huge pollen cloud erupted.

"Whoa!" I cried. "You nearly gave me a heart attack." *Did this tree just sneeze? For real?* "Um, are you okay?"

"I get like this every year around now," the Zeg Tree sighed. "My nose runs, and my eyes itch. I just can't stop... st...ACHOO!" Another pollen cloud exploded from its foliage.

"We call that an allergy," I explained. "You're responding to plant pollen."

"Gah ha ha ha! A tree with a pollen allergy? Don't make me laugh, child of man. Ga hah haa-CHOOOOO!"

"Don't sneeze while you're laughing!" I got it now. Every time the Zeg Tree sneezed, it spread huge quantities of pollen. *If I stop it from sneezing, that'll fix the pollen problem!* The wind would still carry some pollen into Kalta, but not nearly as much.

Kururu and Ririka looked at me, puzzled. I'd have to explain what was happening later.

"Look, I get that you're a tree, but you'd still have an allergic reaction if you came across a type of pollen you had no antibodies for."

"Is that so?" the Zeg Tree inquired. "Nowadays, this forest contains a variety of new plant species, so that theory of yours might be right."

In the end, the Zeg Tree and the residents of Kalta were suffering from the same issue. It was my time to shine.

"Just hang in there!" I urged. "I'll make something that fixes your runny nose and sneezing in no time!"

I turned and started walking away from the great tree.

"What's going on, Reiji?" Ririka asked. "Why were you talking to yourself?"

"The Zeg Tree seems to be struggling with a pollen allergy. I figure I'll make it some meds," I answered.

"A tree has allergies?" Kururu demanded.

"Seems like it."

The elf siblings followed me back to the drugstore. They hung out in the living room, and I headed into the lab, creating a new treatment without much trouble.

> **EXTRA-STRENGTH POLLEN ALLERGY MEDICINE:** Effectively and quickly treats itchy eyes, sneezing, and runny or stuffed-up noses caused by pollen.

Perfect. This should cure the Zeg Tree's allergies! I wasn't sure how much of the medicine I'd need, so I made tons, pouring it into a jug.

I washed my hands in the bathroom, then headed back to the lab. There, I found a black-haired young man kneeling, sipping tea from a familiar-looking cup. He actually looked kind of Japanese. *Who's this guy?*

"You should've told me we had another guest, Mr. Reiji," Mina rebuked me.

"Sorry. Did you serve him that tea, Mina?"

"Of course! I didn't realize that you invited someone besides Kururu and Ririka over. Who is he?"

"Your guess is as good as mine. He's not your friend, right? He definitely isn't Noela's."

If he broke in, he'd have been dealt with by now. Wait... that jug of allergy medicine is gone.

The young man put his teacup down, looking grief-stricken. He picked a headband off the floor, tying it around his head tightly; it was embroidered with the words "extra strength."

"Extra strength"... The missing jug... No way. It can't be. Did that allergy medicine I made become a person? Nah—that's impossible. Right...?

"Um..." I was trying not to panic.

The young man turned to face me, still kneeling. "Ah. Are you the shopkeeper?"

"Uh-huh. So, um, who are you?"

"I'm the allergy medicine you made a few minutes ago," replied the handsome young man wearing the "extra strength" headband.

He's the allergy medicine? But nothing weird happened while I finished that stuff, and I don't think I made a mistake! Did he just appear because I made too much? Is this like how when a bunch of slimes come together, they form a K*ng Slime?

When I used my identification skill, it just repeated "[Extra-Strength Pollen Allergy Medicine]." *Did the allergy treatment...anthropomorphize?*

"Are you wondering how I gained a human body?" Extra Strength smirked, shaking his head. "I'm not sure. But I know you need me to cure the Zeg Tree's allergy."

THAT SEASONAL STUFF

"Yeah, that sums it up." *I was going to tell the Zeg Tree to swallow the medicine—but now it's a* person. *Will that be okay?*

"Might I have some time?" the young man asked.

"Sure! You're really polite for medicine," I said. "I do want to hurry back to the Zeg Tree and fix this pollen issue ASAP, but it'll help if I get you up to speed. By the way, what exactly do you need time to do?"

Extra Strength looked at the lab floor stoically. "I wish to write my will for my mother back home."

"Can you not?!" I groaned. "You're going to make this hard!"

"In that case, I'll write it for my sister."

"You have a sister too?!" *Shouldn't he put* me *in his will?! I'm his father, y'know! The one who made him!*

After he finished writing, the young man turned to me. "I will gladly give my life to serve Kalta by curing the Zeg Tree."

"Don't make this grimmer than it needs to be." I sighed heavily, and we left the drugstore. *Whatever. I've got to use what I have.*

"Your wife seems very kind," Extra Strength mused. "As a young man myself, I can't help feeling envious."

"Mina's my housemate, not my wife."

"Like Mina, my mother is a kind, warm soul."

"Stop with the death flags!" *I guess they're appropriate, though.*

We quickly made our way to the forest. "Watch your feet," I warned.

"Fear not. These paths are nothing compared to the mountain roads of my hometown in the countryside."

"Could you quit talking like a soldier patrolling with his squad in some war movie?"

"My village is a lovely place. The ocean is beautiful."

"I didn't even mention your village."

We walked and talked—although I mostly grumbled. Eventually, we reached the Zeg Tree. The Translator DX was still working, so I was able to communicate with the tree.

"Ah, Sir Reiji," it said. "I've been waiting for you."

"Sorry about the delay. Here's the drugstore's extra-strength allergy medicine." I showed the tree Extra Strength, who—for what it was worth—looked as though he took all this seriously.

"Leave this to me, Reiji," he said. "I'm more than sufficient for curing this tree. Let me...let me go, please!"

"Be my guest," I replied. "That'll make things simple."

Approaching the Zeg Tree, Extra Strength turned to face me, saluting; his strength seemed evident in his face. I returned the salute, although half-heartedly.

THAT SEASONAL STUFF

The Zeg Tree opened its cavernous mouth. "Right here, Sir Reiji!"

"Understood!" I turned back to the young man. "Get in there, Extra Strength!"

"I promise, Reiji, I shall succeed no matter what!"

"I get it! Just go."

"I pray that I, Extra Strength, become a pillar of peace..."

"Kalta's already at peace. You're just treating someone's allergies."

"Tell my family I went honorably!"

"Get going!" I shoved his back.

"Wh-whoa! Don't! What're you thinking?!"

"Enough with the cliched last words! Just go!"

"L-let me do it on my own time! Please!"

"Fine, fine."

"Don't push me, all right?"

"I get it. Just jump in when you're all set."

"I swear I will when I'm ready. So don't push me, no matter what!"

"Jeez. I promise."

WHUMP. I actually did push him.

"Huh?!" Extra Strength disappeared into the Zeg Tree's mouth. I peered inside; the brave-faced young man slowly sank, almost as if he were descending into quicksand.

"Interesting," I remarked. When the only body part visible was Extra Strength's right arm, he slowly clenched his fist, giving me a thumbs-up. "Are you even *trying* to cure this tree's allergies?"

Eventually, the Zeg Tree closed its massive mouth.

"How're you feeling?" I asked.

"Hrm...my nose and eyes are clear, Sir Reiji!"

"Kirio Drugs' products are crazy good, right?" I gave the Zeg Tree a thumbs-up, feeling victorious. I'd been kind of worried about the medication's results, since creating and delivering it had gotten so weird. However, Extra Strength had apparently carried out his task.

Once we'd waited a bit, the tree still had no sniffles and wasn't sneezing; thus, it was no longer spreading huge pollen clouds.

"I'll give your prescription to those two elves," I told the Zeg Tree. "Take it once a day, all right?"

"Of course. Thank you, Sir Reiji!" I turned away from the tree's gruff voice, looking over my shoulder and waving as I headed home.

In my lab, I mixed that same extra-strength allergy medicine repeatedly, but it didn't turn into a person again. *What the hell?*

As I handed Vivi, Mina, and Noela the new treatment, I told them what'd happened.

"That's one of Kirio Drugs' mysteries," Vivi replied, looking perturbed.

"What the heck are the *other* mysteries?" I chuckled.

Mina clasped my hand tightly as the allergy medicine took effect. "My runny nose is gone, Mr. Reiji! I'm not stuffed up, either!"

Noela hugged my waist. "Master! Master!"

"Yeah, yeah. Business as usual."

Kururu and Ririka were still hanging out in the living room. I handed them some allergy meds, telling them to ensure that the Zeg Tree took the treatment daily.

As I'd guessed, Kalta's townspeople had indeed been struggling with pollen allergies; the extra-strength medicine wound up selling like crazy.

DRUGSTORE in another world
~ The Slow Life of a Cheat Pharmacist ~

14
An Olive Branch

When the drugstore emptied out, Ejil turned to me with a guileless expression. "About Noela, Doctor..."

"Hrm? What's up?" *It never turns out well when Ejil approaches me about Noela.*

"Is it possible that she doesn't take me seriously?"

"You just realized that?"

"She should already respect me, right? After all, I'm the demon king."

"Frankly, I don't think she even acknowledges *that*."

"I mean, I'm worried that my friendship with her isn't progressing," Ejil sighed.

"Wow," I said. "You're legit spilling your guts." *Is Ejil saying that he thinks he and Noela are* already *friends? I'm sure she wouldn't say that.* "So you want a closer relationship?"

"I knew you'd understand without me explaining!"

Not long ago, Ejil had impersonated me to mess with Noela. He snuck into her room without permission and did a bunch of other things that raised her hackles. And when I say, "raised her hackles," I mean it—when Ejil worked a shift, Noela did chores with Mina to avoid him.

"Regardless of the world, workplace relationships are rough, huh?" I murmured.

"I'd like a prescription that'll make Noela and me closer, Doctor."

"A prescription can't improve your relationship, bud."

"I don't need her to be my girlfriend! I just want to reach a point where we're less than lovers, but more than friends!"

"I'm not sure I can help with that, Ejil."

"Then how about a prescription for a physical relationship?"

I smacked his head. "You're disgusting."

If I created a product like that, it'd be a mess. *But... hrm...the fact that Ejil brought this up means that, deep down, he understands that he's out of Noela's good graces.*

"I've got it," I told Ejil. "I can't create a product that'll magically improve your relationship with Noela—but I can make something that at least lets you chat as coworkers."

AN OLIVE BRANCH

Ejil gazed at me, teary-eyed. "You always save me in the end, Doctor!"

Frankly, though, I had no plan. "Hang on," I told him.

Entering the house, I found the werewolf girl in the living room. "Hey, Noela. When Ejil's working in the drugstore, you hang out here, right?"

"Arroo? Something wrong with that?"

"Do you hate Ejil?"

Noela went quiet in thought. *How rare.*

"Different from hate."

"Hunh. That's surprising."

"Impossible to stomach Ejil!" Noela said firmly.

Yikes. "Impossible to stomach" is completely different from "hate." Still, when Ejil spoke to Noela, she responded; she'd have ignored him outright if she had zero interest. *But what exactly does not being able to "stomach" him mean? People in Japan say that kind of thing a lot.* On a personal level, I saw it as dislike for someone's appearance, movements, expressions, scent, hygiene, speech patterns—that kind of stuff.

"What exactly can you not stomach?" I sat next to Noela on the sofa.

She plopped down in my lap as usual, wagging her nice, fluffy tail. "Silly laugh. Too confident."

Well, he rules the monster and demon folk. I understand why he's got a big head and idiotic laugh.

"Can't stomach flirting," Noela added.

"Ha ha...probably because you've written him off."

"Also, Ejil no smell like Master," she concluded.

"Probably because he's a demon," I pointed out. "I don't know much about people's odors, but you can smell the difference between Ejil and me, right?"

Noela nodded. "Like Master's smell. Hate Ejil's."

That might be pheromone-related. Like how girls can't handle their dad's B.O. after a certain point. "Gotcha. Thanks." Noela seemed bewildered as I moved her off my lap.

I made my way to the lab and started working immediately. *People have genetic affinities for certain scents. If I create a product using the DNA of someone whose smell Noela likes—me—that should work.* I shook the bottle, finishing the unique formula.

KR'S GENETIC JUICE: Beverage containing Kirio Reiji's DNA.

Perfect. If Ejil ingests this, he'll absorb my genetic sequence. And what people eat affects their body odor, so this was all working out quite nicely. I headed back to the drugstore.

"Listen, you won't get anything out of this product right off the bat," I told Ejil. "Put it in your food for about

AN OLIVE BRANCH

a week, and it'll change your DNA so you smell like somebody Noela likes." I handed him the new product.

"A-amazing, Doctor! How can I possibly repay you?!"

"Don't mention it. It's an employer's job to keep the workplace friendly."

"I'll follow you until my last breath, Doctor!"

"Yeah, yeah, I know." I calmed the overwrought Ejil down.

For the next seven days, Ejil carefully used the genetic juice as I'd instructed. I couldn't tell you what changed, but Noela was immediately confused, often looking from me to Ejil as if comparing us. After a week, the fluid ran out, and I decided to figure out whether Ejil's scent was like mine with Mina's help.

"The first annual 'Guess Which Scent Is Reiji's!' contest begins now!" Mina, the experiment's emcee, announced excitedly. She held a ladle like a microphone, and her face grew redder by the second. "Woo-hoo!"

"What wrong, Mina?"

"Has something happened, woman?" Ejil demanded.

"Hey, Mina? You can be yourself for this."

"Y-you should've said so!" Mina blushed. "Now I look like a weirdo who freaked out about nothing!"

"You didn't just *look* like one."

"Oh, gosh. Enough." She crouched, overwhelmed by embarrassment.

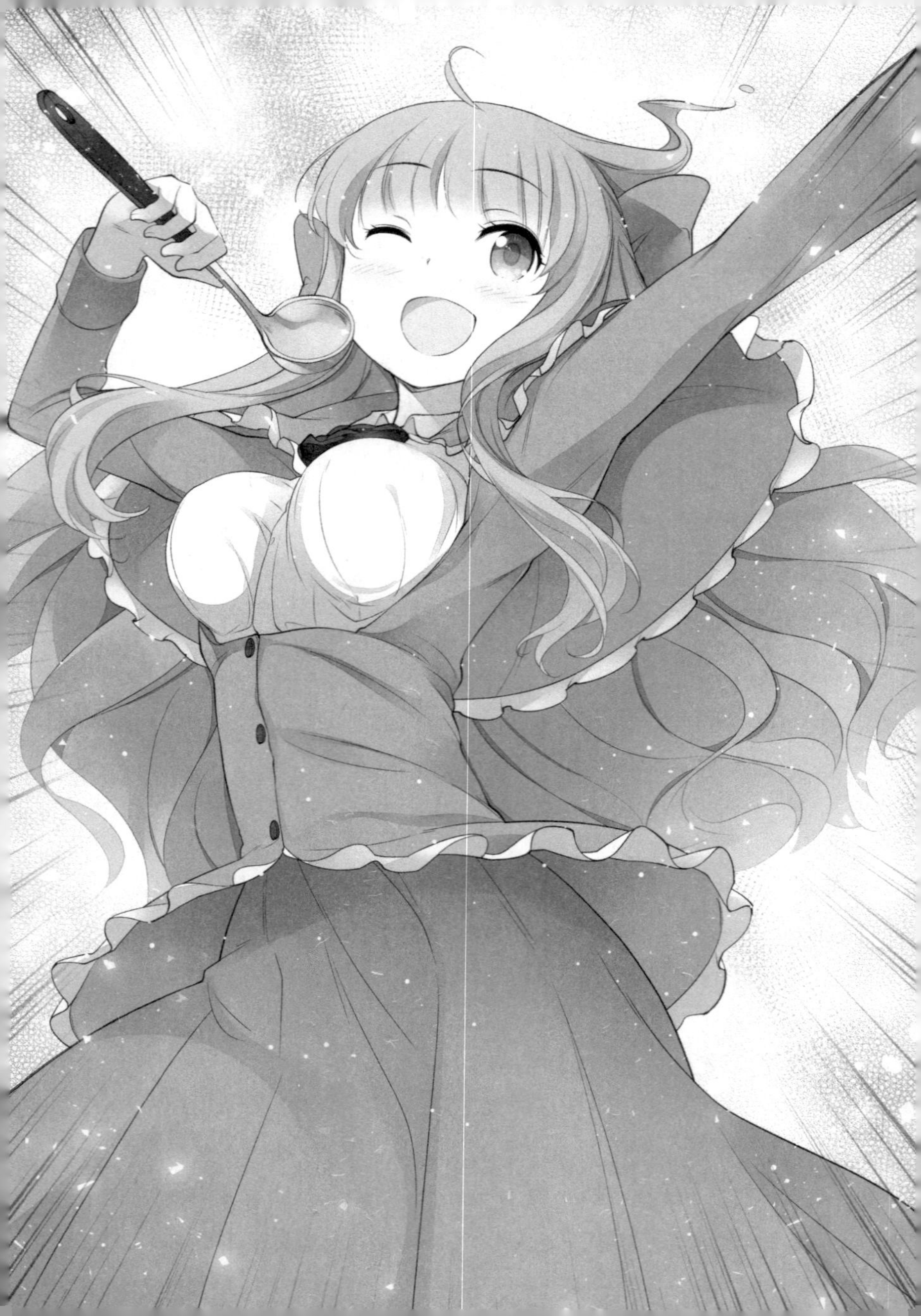

AN OLIVE BRANCH

Since Mina was beside herself, I stepped up to explain the test to Ejil and Noela. "I'm going to dump the formula on Ejil, myself, and this tomato." Tomatoes were Noela's least favorite food. "Then Noela will sniff out which one is me."

"Garoo!" Noela looked at me confidently. "Noela never mistake Master."

That was partly thanks to visual information—which was why this test would be blind. "Okay, Noela, close your eyes."

Mina blindfolded the werewolf girl. "You shouldn't be able to see in front of you now," she told Noela, checking to ensure that was the case.

"What ladle for, Mina?" Noela demanded. "First annual contest? Will there be second?"

Don't torture her anymore, Noela! You can't see that Mina's so embarrassed, she's half crying!

Ejil and I put boxes over our heads, and we covered the plated tomato with a box. Since Noela was going to sniff the boxes, Mina made sure the werewolf girl didn't peek. Ejil and I shuffled around and swapped places, then rested the boxes covering our heads on the table.

Box A contained the genetic-juice-drenched tomato—Noela's worst enemy. Box B covered Ejil's head, and Box C was me. Guided by Mina, Noela thrust her nose at each box. Ejil said nothing; since this was the moment of truth, his poise was exceptionally self-disciplined and stoic.

Noela sniffed Box C, tilting her head. "Garr...roooo?"

Heh heh! And she was so full of confidence.

In terms of scent, there wasn't much that distinguished Ejil from me, which meant the genetic juice worked quite effectively.

"Can you tell which box is Mr. Reiji, Noela?" Mina inquired.

"C? B...? Garroo..." Noela sniffed the boxes in order again. "Know it!"

"Then please tell us your answer."

"Master in Box C!"

Mina untied Noela's blindfold, and Noela pounced on the right answer—in other words, me. *But, hey, the genetic-juice formula still worked like I hoped.*

"Noela guess right!" the werewolf girl declared. "Praise Noela, Master!"

"You bet." I stroked her head gently.

The usually overbearing Ejil simply placed Box B on the table and looked toward the sky. He closed his eyes in disappointment.

He had a lot riding on this, I reflected. "I could tell you weren't totally sure at first, Noela."

AN OLIVE BRANCH

"Yes," agreed Mina. "What gave Mr. Reiji away?"

"Wasn't sure if B or C!" Noela explained. "But at end, B breathe heavy."

Wait. He did?

"Knew right away, Ejil," she concluded.

"When Noela sniffed me so resolutely, I couldn't stop myself," the demon king sighed.

I'm changing my mind about him being stoic. "You're just a pervert."

"But your new product is the real deal, Doctor!" Ejil insisted. "If I apply it daily, Noela will sniff me every single time! Bwa ha ha ha!"

Noela looked as though she was staring at a pile of garbage. "This side of Ejil, can't stomach," she snapped.

"Bwa ha ha! I smell like the good doctor now, Noela!" Ejil spread his arms, beckoning her.

She smacked him with her tail. "Hate Ejil!"

"Bwaah—?!"

This is no good. Changing Ejil's scent won't patch things up. It's true that Noela can't stomach his natural odor, but he has tons of other flaws.

So I explained the demon king's motivations. "Hey, Noela, Ejil wants to be friends with you." I told her simply that, since we all worked at the drugstore, it'd be great if we were on good terms.

"Make sense." Noela seemed to grasp the situation. She shook Ejil's hand, silent and seemingly embarrassed.

"Noela..." Ejil looked close to tears. "So this is what it means to be in love with a minx!"

"Ejil, this why can't stomach."

Nevertheless, Ejil and Noela got just a bit closer that day.

15

Sleep Versus Endless Rest

OH, CRAP. I screwed up. Mina was in my bed, fast asleep. *What should I do?*

"M-Mina...?" She showed no sign of waking.

I was in something of a panic when I heard the door open. "Where Mina, Master?"

I hurriedly covered her with my blanket. "Sh-sh-she w-went shopping. Yeah!"

"Got it." Noela trotted out.

That was way too close. Not that it'd be a huge deal if Noela saw Mina in here, but... Wait, would *it be?* I couldn't judge this situation properly. In fact, I'd panicked so hard, I'd fibbed to Noela.

"H-hey, Mina. Lovely little Mina?" No response. "If you don't wake up, I'll flip your skirt."

Still no response. She was fast asleep.

"Augh! Mina, how long do you plan to snooze for?!"

◆◆◆

Last night, Mina had come to me with something on her mind. "I haven't been able to sleep recently," she'd told me. "I'm so tired, I can barely focus on work or chores."

"That's got to be rough."

Mina said that even the drugstore's bubble bath didn't help. *I guess that makes sense. The bubble bath just enhances bedtime. Being warm helps you nod off, but it doesn't actually make you sleepy.*

"Could there be a problem with my bed or blankets?" Mina inquired.

"Wanna try a different bed? I'll use yours, and you can sleep in mine."

We gave it a shot, but Mina still couldn't doze off. That night, she shook me awake.

"Sorry to wake you like this, Mr. Reiji."

"Still can't sleep?"

She shook her head apologetically.

Mina helped a lot at the drugstore and always did her best with the housework. Insomnia might really bother her, and if it did, the domino effect would make things

SLEEP VERSUS ENDLESS REST

tough for Noela and me too. I needed to do everything I could to help her sleep.

"Let me see if I can make a simple treatment," I offered.

"Thank you, but it's late. It can wait until tomorrow."

"Nah, that's fine. I'm already wide awake," I replied, heading to the lab.

I wasn't making something complicated with tons of rare ingredients, so it didn't take me long to finish up.

SLEEPY SLEEP: Sleep aid. No side effects. Suitable for small children.

Figuring that that would get Mina to sleep, I went back to my room and found her in my bed. Ideally, she would've drifted off while I concocted the sleepy-sleep treatment. Unfortunately, reality hadn't worked that way.

I heard Mina sniff. "Smells like Mr. Reiji..."

Why's she smelling my bed?

"I sort of feel as though I'm doing something I shouldn't," she murmured to herself. "My heart's racing."

"You're never gonna get to sleep doing that."

"Eek! M-Mr. Reiji! Wh-what is it?"

"I made your prescription. Here."

"F-for the record, I certainly haven't been lying here,

smelling your bed," Mina stammered. "I just couldn't sleep, so I got curious!"

"It's fine. Please don't explain yourself." She probably hadn't lied about her insomnia; I'd seen bags under her eyes these last few days. I handed her the brand-new formula. "I fine-tuned it so it's safe for kids. Its effect on adults may be mild." *On the other hand, whenever I make a product, it always works too well.* "Don't drink the whole thing. Just take a sip, okay?"

"All right." Mina drank about half the bottle's contents.

I definitely told her only to take a sip! "You should be fine now. Let me know if you still can't sleep."

"I will. Thanks so much, Mr. Reiji."

After we said goodnight, I made my way back to Mina's bedroom; Noela was already fast asleep.

◆◆◆

This morning, Mina still wasn't awake. I left her alone until noon, since she hadn't been sleeping much. Now it was lunchtime, and she still showed no sign of waking up.

Jeez, what am I supposed to do? What if Mina never gets up again?!

"Wait...wouldn't that be my fault? After all, a drugstore product knocked her out. Mina, please! Wake! Up!"

SLEEP VERSUS ENDLESS REST

Grabbing her shoulders, I shook her as hard as I could, but she was still fast asleep.

That evening, there was no change in Mina's condition. Noela and I had dinner out; needless to say, she continued to dream even after we returned. *This isn't good.*

Looking at the unconscious Mina, Noela said with certainty, "Mina wake if tummy hurt, for sure."

"Uh, really? I mean, I doubt that'd be enough to…"

"Tummy hurt if put pill in butt."

"You mean a suppository?!" I gaped at Noela. "Y-you'd handle that, right?"

"Impossible."

"Yo! Mina! *Wake up*!" I shook her shoulders again and even pinched her cheeks. "If you don't, I might have to prescribe a suppository!"

It was no good. There was zero sign of Mina regaining consciousness. As I yelled at the sleeping beauty, Noela turned to fetch a suppository from the drugstore.

"Hold on, Noela! Let's have Mina drink tons of water and see whether she wakes up to use the bathroom," I suggested. "Your plan…definitely isn't tentative, but it's possible Mina would never speak to me again."

I filled a pitcher and, bit by bit, helped Mina drink a liter of water. There was a good chance she'd just wet the bed. But since I didn't want to invade her privacy, this was the safest strategy by far—and the only one that prevented anyone from being hurt.

Noela and I headed back to the girls' bedroom and went to sleep, hoping Mina would wake up the next morning.

Mina finally regained consciousness just after noon and dropped into the drugstore. Her face was well-rested, her skin silky-smooth. "Goodness, I slept so well! Thank you, Mr. Reiji."

"G-great," I stammered. "I'm so... so glad you're awake. I mean it. Otherwise, I would've gone on my last mission tonight."

"Hrm?" Mina looked at the clock. "Oh, but I've overslept a bit! It's already after lunch."

"Today's the *fourth*, Mina."

"Huh? You mean the third, right?"

"Uh-uh. Over thirty hours have passed since you took that sleepy-sleep formula."

"Wha—?! B-but..."

"What's wrong?"

"Uh...um...n-nothing. Ah ha ha!"

Mina was clearly hiding something. I was puzzled over what it could be, but I decided not to let it frustrate me. Later that night, after she shook me awake, I discovered what she was concealing.

"Hrm...what's up, Mina?"

"Um...I still can't sleep, Mr. Reiji."

"Seriously? Well...if I prescribe some sleepy-sleep, and you dilute it with water, it should work fine."

Mina seemed to struggle to find the right words. "To be honest, last night...I got up to use the bathroom."

"Huh?" *I guess my water plan worked.* "That means..."

"On top of that, when I woke up this morning, I just curled up in your bed, and..."

"Nodded off? You're telling me you went back to bed *again*? Well, well. You sure enjoyed your beauty sleep, huh?"

"Tee hee!" Mina giggled.

"Don't you 'tee hee' me! Do you realize how worried I was?"

"I'm sorry! Um...could I have some of that sleepy-sleep medicine tonight too?"

"It sounds like you don't regret sleeping late at all." I pointed at her. "I'm prescribing you a *suppository*!"

"E-excuse me?! Those go in your *butt*, right?!" She balked. "You'll see everything!"

"It's for your health! No point in resisting!"

"I requested the sleepy-sleep formula!"

"For Little Miss Sleepyhead who goes back to sleep *twice,* that formula is prescribed alongside a suppository.

If you don't want to suffer through it, you'll have to fall asleep by yourself. You better remember that!"

By sunrise, Mina hadn't drifted off; she'd basically already overslept. She wasn't the least bit tired, though, thanks to all the rest she got the previous night.

I diluted the sleepy-sleep formula before putting it on sale. It proved especially effective for insomnia patients and sleepless, crying children; it sold particularly well to married couples.

16
Smoopy-Doopy Skin

IT WAS WARMING UP in Kalta now that the sun was out longer. The weather wasn't impossible to deal with—it wasn't nearly as humid as Japan—but the sun was still as strong as hell.

As I rested my chin on the counter, Vivi tugged my shirt. "Reiji! Reiji!"

"Hey, lake fairy. Man, it's nice and cool when you're nearby."

"Tee hee! I need to stay cold all the time, so—hey! I'm a *spirit*, not a fairy!" Vivi punched me lightly several times; it didn't hurt.

"What's the matter, Miss Spirit?"

"Well...I've spent most of my life either in the lake or under trees," Vivi said. "So, I'm pretty sensitive to sunlight."

"Hunh. Is that so?"

"Ugh! You can't pretend to be interested?" Vivi pouted. "Anyway, you understand what I'm saying, right?"

"Uh...you need to go home early? That's fine. It's not busy today."

"Stop trying to get me to leave! That isn't what I meant!"

"Then spit it out!"

"This might have to do with my skin tone, but when I'm in strong sunlight..."

"You melt?"

"I wouldn't be here if I melted!" Vivi yelled, swinging both arms at me. Needless to say, the blows didn't hurt in the least. As usual, teasing her was a blast. "In strong sunlight, my skin starts to sting," she finished.

I looked at Vivi's face; she was ruddier than usual. The backs of her hands were red too. "You can go home early."

"Stop trying to send me home!" she yelped. "You know I look forward to working! I can't just go back to the lake!"

"Right. I forgot—all you have waiting for you is your pet goblin."

"He's not a pet. And he's not at the lake either!" she snapped. "He had to go train, and he hasn't been back for ages. Urgh—that's beside the point!"

"So your skin's sensitive to the sun, and you want me to do something about that?"

SMOOPY-DOOPY SKIN

"If you understand, stop trying to change the subject!"

"My bad." I patted her head apologetically. Teasing Vivi was so fun, I sometimes went overboard. "I'm happy to try to keep you from getting sunburnt. Still, nothing's wrong with a nice brown tan."

Vivi's skin was a fantastically pure white. By human standards, she hardly looked healthy.

"Well, I'd like to have the same complexion as Mina, if possible," she said. We took it for granted, but Mina was in fact a ghost, so she was obviously pale too.

"Then you'll need a product for UV protection," I replied.

"Will you make something?"

"Sure. We've got no customers."

"Yay! Thanks, Reiji!"

I left the store to Noela and Vivi, heading for the lab. Just as I started working, Mina brought me some tea. "What're you making this time?"

"Vivi asked for a product to prevent sunburn."

"You can make that?"

"Well, it won't protect your skin 100 percent, but it'll make a big difference."

"I'm sure that'll sell like crazy! Women all over want to avoid sunburn. Good luck, Mr. Reiji!" Mina cheered me on as she left the lab, looking overjoyed.

She'd also brought me some snacks; I ate them gratefully as I wrapped up my work.

> **SUNSCREEN**: Protects against UV rays. Helps prevent sunburns. Washes off.

Perfect. Done!

As I poured the gel into a wide-mouthed bottle, Mina and Vivi rushed in with perfect timing.

"You're finished, Mr. Reiji?"

"All done, Reiji?!"

They must've been spying on me from the doorway. I knew I felt eyes on me. "Calm yourselves, fair ladies. The first one to test this sunscreen will be…"

Both young women immediately knelt and raised their hands. *They must be dying to use this stuff!* I put the sunscreen bottle between them; their faces lit up as if they were children who'd just found treasure. *Seeing them this thrilled makes formulating a new product worthwhile.*

As simply as possible, I explained how to use the sunscreen. "Put a little on your finger, then spread it over the area exposed to the sun."

Vivi and Mina nodded, listening carefully. Following my instructions, they rubbed sunscreen on their arms, hands, and faces.

"It's nice and cool!" Mina exclaimed.

"Mm-hmm! My skin feels soft."

They headed out to sunbathe right away.

"Oh, gosh!" Vivi called from outside. "This is amazing, Reiji! The sunlight isn't bothering me!"

"Good to hear."

Noela tugged my sleeve, puzzled by Vivi's excitement. "What wrong with Vivi, Master?"

"Oh, she's pumped because I made sunscreen."

"Noela use too!"

"Er...seriously? I mean, that's fine, but it's kind of surprising."

Noela snorted and retrieved the sunscreen.

Meanwhile, Mina came in to question me about Noela's demand. "Frankly, I'm surprised," she admitted. "Noela doesn't strike me as the type to be interested in skincare."

"My thoughts exactly," I replied. "She usually only has eyes for food."

"She must be that age." Mina sounded like an elder sister watching a sibling mature.

Vivi rushed in too. "Reiji, come here! Touch my skin! It's smoopy-doopy!"

What the hell does that even mean?

She patted her cheeks gently, so I did the same.

"It *is* smoopy-doopy! Your cheeks feel awesome!" I exclaimed. *I could get addicted to this!*

"Wait a sec," I added. "You start work at the drugstore in the morning, and you leave after dark, right? You spend the whole day in here. Why're you terrified of sunlight if you're barely in it?"

"Uh..."

"You seriously didn't think about that?" I teased as I cupped Vivi's cheeks.

Noela grabbed my arm. "Noela too, Master!"

"Huh? Oh, uh, sure." I patted Noela's face just like Vivi's.

Mina nodded as she watched. "Now it's all clear to me," she giggled, heading from the storefront to the house.

What exactly is clear to her?

Vivi ate dinner with us, and I walked her to the town gate.

"Thank you so much for the sunscreen, Reiji! Now I can stay in the sun without worrying."

"Says the spirit who spends her time in the shade or at work."

"Why do you have to say stuff like that? Keep it to yourself!"

"Well, at any rate, you can't use the sun as an excuse for days off now," I ribbed her. "All's well that ends well."

"Bye!" Vivi waved and left.

SMOOPY-DOOPY SKIN

When I got home, Noela pushed her face into me. "Touch, Master! Squishy."

"You sure are. Your skin feels awesome."

"Garroo!" Noela dived onto the couch, tail wagging happily. Mina couldn't help giggling.

"Hey, Mina, what exactly was 'all clear' to you earlier? Was it something about Noela?"

"Yes. It was quite simple," Mina admitted. "You know Noela and Vivi are very close, don't you?"

"Of course. So?"

"Well, you flattered Vivi a ton. Noela couldn't put up with that, especially since Vivi's her dear friend."

"That's why she used the sunscreen too?"

"She was a bit envious," Mina confirmed.

"I get it now," I told her, but I didn't quite understand why Noela had been jealous.

"That's how women are," Mina added, but I was still kind of lost.

Later, the drugstore started carrying the sunscreen, and it sold like hotcakes to young women and wives in particular. It was no exaggeration to say it caused a long-term skincare craze in Kalta.

DRUGSTORE in another world
~ The Slow Life of a Cheat Pharmacist ~

17
Herding Cats

"**N**o bug Master. Here!"

Noela beckoned to the cat. It paid her no mind, trotting toward the drugstore's front entrance and curling up.

"Urgh. No listen, Master!"

"What've I been telling you?"

"Use werewolf power to force!" Noela cried.

What's she planning?

The werewolf girl leapt at the cat. It freaked out and bit her, its fur standing on end.

"Master...hurts."

"I know, I know." I patted Noela's head. "Have a potion."

"Arroo!" Her ears shot straight up. Grabbing a potion from inside the drugstore, she opened the bottle.

Was that her goal all along?

Mina popped out from the house. "You're both still going at it? It's just a cute little kitty cat, Mr. Reiji. Can't we let it be?"

"No, we can't."

Honestly, I liked cats, but they'd bother customers if they wandered around outside the drugstore. Sure, there were folks who'd be fine with the critters, but they'd also drive others away. Anyway, letting feral animals prowl nearby wouldn't be great for the store's reputation.

"Here! No annoy Master!" Noela tried her best to lure the cat away from the door. No luck.

The biggest problem? We'd gone from one cat to two, and then to three. Their numbers kept rising. The issue had started about a week before, after Noela fed a stray in the neighborhood.

"Don't give it too much now," I'd warned her.

"Kitty cold, Master. Empty tummy. Noela save."

She'd been really passionate about it. But the stray cat had warmed to her, and now a bunch of cats hung out here. They seem attached to Noela; that would've been great if they'd obeyed her, but I'm sure you know how those little dudes can be. They probably just saw her as their food-delivery girl.

There are seriously already five cats chilling out here. Jeez, how'd we attract so many? As far as I knew, there were only two strays in the neighborhood before.

"Wow! Look at all these cute little kitties!" Mina's face wore a big, warm smile.

I was pretty sure Mina was also a guilty party; she'd probably fed the cats a ton after she saw Noela do it.

"Girls, what do you say to looking after these little guys in the house?"

Mina and Noela gaped at me.

"Just to be clear, Noela," I added, "if we do that, I won't be your master anymore. I'll be the stray cats' master."

"Arroo?! No! Big problem!"

"I can only be one species' master at a time," I insisted.

Noela tried to catch a black cat she'd doted on earlier. "Black Tiger!"

"Black Tiger"? Like the Japanese shrimp? Of all the names to choose. I mean, yeah, it is *black... and* tigers *are* felines. Technically, it made perfect sense.

Mina didn't lift a finger to help shoo the animals away. And, although Noela didn't want to lose her master to a bunch of cats, the strays would just return if we took them someplace else.

Plus, I feel bad chasing them off. But the drugstore's gonna become a cat cafe! What can I do here? "Come to think of it," I muttered, "we don't have any of *that*."

I guess I'll make some. I'd doubted whether it qualified as a "drugstore product," but my medicine-making skill was responding, so that settled it.

"Can you watch the shop for me, Mina?" I called.

"Sure thing!"

It didn't look as though any customers would swing by, so Mina would be fine. I glanced at Noela; it turned out she'd admitted defeat. She was just playing with the cats now.

You give up way too easily, Noela! Man, she's hopeless.

I headed to the lab. Not much seafood was sold in Kalta, unlike Japan. If I used that to my advantage, though, I might be able to fool the stray cats—in a good way.

I mixed the simple formula and shook the bottle. It glowed, signaling that the product was finished.

IRRESISTIBLE TUNA SCENT

Okay. If I put some of this on the cats' food...

I heard footsteps outside.

"Aw! You can't go in."

"Black Tiger!"

What's going on out there?

Something clawed at the lab door. *Scratch! Scratch!* I opened the door slowly.

Fwoosh! The black cat leapt right onto my face. "Meeeow!"

"What the—?!" I fell on my butt.

The rest of the cats were apparently lurking nearby; they leapt on me too.

"Meeeow!"

"Mrooooow!"

"Purrrrr!"

The stray cats licked my fingers. *What's going on?! Oh—they must smell my latest creation!* I had the bottle sealed, though. Was its faint scent still enough to get the cats this excited?

"Mr. Reiji's covered in kitties!" Mina exclaimed. She rushed into the lab, trying to capture the strays.

"Mreeeooooow!"

They really don't like that. Is Mina the type cats don't take to?

"Okay, Master?"

"Uh-huh. But I saw those cats going ballistic firsthand."

"Mreeeeeooooow!" The cats in Mina's arms were freaking out. They almost sounded like they were yelling for her to let them go.

"Aw. I want to be as popular with these kitties as you are," Mina sighed. "Why do they hate me so much now? They're calm when I feed them."

That's because they see you as a food-delivery woman. And I knew you fed them! Yet seeing Mina so sad made me sympathize.

Noela sniffed at me intently. "Good smell, Master!"

I handed her the bottle of irresistible tuna scent. "Put a bit of this on top of whatever you feed the cats."

"Got it!" Noela trotted to the kitchen.

Hrm. I bet she'll feed them our leftover chicken or something.

However, she soon returned and shook her head. "This no good, Master."

"Er, why not?"

"Only smell good. No taste," she said with a serious expression. "Need salt."

"You ate some, didn't you, Noela?"

"No..."

"Then how do you know what it tastes like?"

Noela fell silent. Sweat started to trickle down her forehead.

"It's not salad dressing." Ultimately, it didn't matter whether the product was tasteless. It was just supposed to *smell* really good to the strays—although apparently, even Noela thought it smelled great. At any rate, salt isn't good for cats.

To ensure that Noela didn't sneak any more of the

tuna scent, I accompanied her to the kitchen, sprinkling the liquid on the cats' food myself.

From the lab, I heard Mina's voice. "Eek! Stop thrashing!"

"Let's go somewhere nice and open," I suggested to Noela. Rather than letting the stray cats hang out in front of the drugstore, we'd lure them someplace out of the way.

Noela and I exited the shop, both carrying dishes of tuna-scented food.

"Mreeoooow!" The cats rushed after us, panicked.

Whoa! "Hurry, Noela!"

"Leave it to Noela!" *Crunch!* "No taste."

"Stop eating the bait!" I grabbed the food from Noela's hands, sprinting toward an open area.

Rumble! It almost sounded like the ground behind us was shaking.

"Look, Master!"

I turned around. Lo and behold, a pack of stray cats chased us, eyes sparkling with desire. It would've been fine if we were just facing two or three, but literally dozens of cats were approaching. Frankly, it was terrifying.

Noela and I finally reached the clearing. I put the two plates of tuna-scented food in the center before darting away.

"MREEEOOOOOW!"

The cats assaulted the plates with violent fervor. In the circle of strays was a single black cat. "Black Tiger!" Noela cried.

The cat ran toward her, rubbing against her legs affectionately. "Mrow. Meow!"

Like Noela, I scratched Black Tiger on the chin before leaving the strays behind. Fortunately, none followed us.

At the drugstore, I set a rule that employees who wanted to feed the cats had to do it at the clearing. That way, they'd stop waiting for us to feed them outside the drugstore.

"Even I'll be popular with the cats now!" Mina declared that evening, during dinner.

"Noela play with Black Tiger!" Noela proclaimed.

They'd seemingly gone beyond being the cats' food-delivery women.

Once I put the irresistible tuna scent on sale, it sold well to cat lovers from Kalta and elsewhere; they rushed to the drugstore in droves. But that wasn't all. Customers loved that the formula smelled like fresh fish, since seafood wasn't readily available, and restaurants and households bought it in bulk. It became a crazy-popular product across the board.

18

A Real Ladies' Man

"**H**UH? ME? But why?" I couldn't help whining.

Elaine sat across from me. She puffed out her flat chest. "Mother and Father said you'd be great!"

"I don't even know how to act at an aristocrats' party. Can't you pick someone else?"

"Absolutely not."

I didn't do well at big parties. It wasn't that I disliked talking to strangers, but it was draining. *Plus, we're talking nobility.* If I said or did something rude, it'd be bad.

"You're famous in all the towns Father rules," Elaine added.

"In *all* of Lord Valgas's towns?" Elaine's dad was Lord Casti something-or-other Valgas. His full name was so long, I frequently forgot it.

Elaine's declaration at least gave me a clearer picture

of things. Lord Valgas wanted to invite Kirio Drugs' owner to the party to brag about my accomplishments. *Can't say I'm a fan of being a tool for his little plot.*

"If you attend, it'll be good publicity for the drugstore," Elaine told me as I hesitated.

"I'm not exactly looking to do more business."

"There'll be lots of delicious food."

"I eat plenty of good food these days."

"Gosh, why're you being so stubborn?!" She'd finally snapped at me, provoked by my clear indifference to her invitation.

"Stubborn? You're the one trying to make me go to this party."

"All the attendees use the drugstore's products. They want to express their gratitude!"

Hmm. Frankly, no one hates praise. I was weak to that kind of thing. Plus, I was eager to learn which treatments the nobles bought. "Fine, I'll go. Happy?"

Elaine lit up. "Fear not, Sir Reiji! I'll stay by your side all night, ensuring that you don't make a gaffe."

"Right. I'll be counting on you."

Elaine clapped, and an older gentleman entered the drugstore. "I've brought your attire, Sir Kirio." He carried a button-down shirt, necktie, and suit—the right outfit for blending in at the aristocrats' gathering.

Wow, talk about prepared.

"I shall call for you in three days," Elaine told me. "When the time comes, please wear those."

"Got it."

Having accomplished her objective, Elaine headed back to the carriage in high spirits, and she and the old servant returned home.

"If Elaine sticks around and gives me instructions, I should make it through this get-together in one piece," I mused.

Still, I'd have been lying if I'd said I was no longer concerned. Plus, the suit I'd received filled me with the same sense of foreboding I'd had when I got my first job.

Vivi entered the drugstore, having finished her break. "What's wrong, Reiji? If you're in trouble, you know you can talk to me, right? I'm a lake spirit, after all!"

"I appreciate you worrying about me, but I'm fine."

"Really?"

Patting Vivi gently on the head, I asked her to watch the drugstore so I could try on the suit. *Hunh. It fits perfectly. It's definitely not a hand-me-down either—it's got to be brand-new.* The Valgas family must've had it tailored for me. They really were planning to bring me to this party come hell or high water. I looked at myself in the mirror. *Seems okay.*

"Eek!" Mina's brief scream made me stare at her. She covered her face with her hands. "I-I'm so sorry! I didn't realize you were changing. My peeping was a happy coincidence!"

"Happy, huh?"

"Forget I said anything!" Blushing, Mina carefully inspected my new outfit. "Why're you dressed up, Mr. Reiji? Not that you don't look great in a suit!"

"Thanks." I then explained the situation.

"I see," Mina replied. "I suppose it's not a stretch to say you're a household name. I'm sure Lord Valgas will love bragging about you. Have fun!" She hurried out.

I glanced in the mirror again. The suit was fine, but something felt off—maybe because it'd been a while since I last dressed formally. I thought back to weekday mornings on Earth.

"Oh, right!" Just like that, I solved the riddle. I didn't have any of *that* stuff here in Kalta. "Might as well whip some up now. I don't need any special ingredients."

I left Vivi to watch the store while I worked in the lab. *When it comes to dressing up, you can't complete your look without this stuff!*

♦︎♦︎♦︎

Three days later, Elaine glanced at me in the rocking carriage. "M-my heart's racing!"

Pop! She blushed.

Why "pop"? I wondered.

"You look rather dashing," the girl continued. "Your face looks manlier than usual!"

"My face definitely hasn't changed," I replied. *My hairstyle, on the other hand...*

Three days back, I'd concocted some strong-hold wax to fix my hair up. Judging by Elaine's reaction, I must've been rocking the look. I figured she was especially surprised because I usually had bedhead at the drugstore. This was the first time I'd tidied my hair in this world, let alone used actual hair wax. *The me from my businessman days is back in action!*

"This is bad," Elaine muttered.

"What is?"

"Well, quite a few young women like myself will attend the party."

"Is that so?"

"It *is* so! Don't you understand what I mean?!"

Why is Drills getting so loud? I couldn't make heads or tails of her words until we arrived at the venue.

◆♦◆

"Greetings, Sir Reiji! It's been quite some time." Lord Valgas and I shook hands.

I greeted Lady Flam as well. "Good evening. Thank you for having me."

She laughed as you'd imagine a noblewoman laughing. "You clean up well, Sir Alchemist!"

Could you please stop calling me that?

I could tell the atmosphere at the soiree had changed; I was turning heads all over the chamber.

A young woman in a pretty gown spoke to me despite her nervousness. "Um...are you Sir Kirio of Kirio Drugs?"

"Uh, yeah, that's correct."

She told me she used the drugstore's hair products regularly. "Ever since I started, my hair's been wonderfully silky!"

"Really? Glad to hear it."

I could feel the girls at the party gazing passionately at me. They all had drill-like ringlets like Elaine's.

"So, that youth is Sir Kirio?"

"The genius alchemist who developed the beauty gel?"

"What a dashing young man! I must say hello!"

"I'm wearing charm fragrance tonight—I wonder whether I could get a word with him."

Come to think of it, I've formulated a bunch of stuff that's popular with young women—shampoo, a hair mask, conditioner, perfume, and beauty gel.

A REAL LADIES' MAN

The shampoo girl didn't seem to be going anywhere, so another young lady cut in. "Excuse me. I'd like a word with Sir Kirio. Sir Kirio, I'm the Nesta family's second daughter, and—"

As she attempted to offer a curtsy, another young lady interrupted. "Might I introduce myself as well?"

"Hey, don't cut in line!"

Another girl appeared. "Could I have a moment?"

"Me as well!"

"And me!"

"Whoa, hey, hold on!" The army of young women was crushing me. The quantity of drill curls in my vicinity was absurdly high.

"I knew this would happen!" Another set of drills got between me and the girls; this time, the curls belonged to the one and only Elaine. "Leave this to me, Sir Reiji!"

"You got it!" *An eye for an eye, a drill for a drill...whatever that means.*

"Excuse me! Who are you?"

"Could you step aside?"

"Enough!"

All the girls spoke the same way; I could only distinguish them by voice and appearance. At any rate, Elaine had somehow managed to deter the incoming young women.

"Gah ha ha ha!" laughed Lord Valgas. "With looks and pharmaceutical skills like yours, any young woman of any house would gladly wed you."

Once I'd done the rounds of the party, my role was apparently finished. Lady Flam clapped, summoning a carriage for me. As I got in, I heard young women squealing my name. "Sir Kirio!"

Is this what it means to be a ladies' man?

♦ ♦ ♦

A few days later, several love letters addressed to me arrived at Kirio Drugs. As I wrote a response to each one, Noela and Mina entered the lab.

"No, Master!"

"Noela's right, Mr. Reiji. Th-this is awful."

Both women looked melancholy, but neither told me what I was doing wrong. It wasn't like I wanted to court the young noblewomen; frankly, I couldn't even tell them apart. I felt bad about it, but I'd been cranking out rejection letters using a template I'd made.

At any rate, my suit-and-waxed-hair look had scored big with Mina and Noela.

19
Stopping the Shocks

As I REFORMULATED a treatment we were low on, I heard a scream from the drugstore. "Kyaaaaah!"

Vivi...? Why's she screaming? Eh, she and Noela were watching the store. They're probably just up to something.

"What're you doing, Noela?!" I heard Vivi shriek.

"Arroo? Nothing!"

I assumed they were just messing around, but something still seemed odd. Curious, I poked my head into the drugstore. "What's going on in here?"

"Ah—Reiji! Listen!" Vivi had tears in her eyes.

The two approached me; Noela seemed panicked. "No! Noela not know! Serious, Master!"

Okay, what's wrong, ladies?

"I thought Noela was my friend!" Vivi whimpered. "She did something awful!"

"No, Vivi! Noela not know! Realest really. Believe, Master!" Noela was now teary as well.

I stroked their heads gently. I refused to believe Noela would hurt a friend without reason. "I'm not seeing the full picture here. What do you mean by 'awful,' Vivi?"

"I'm not sure, but when I went by her, I think she slapped me!"

"You *think*? You don't know if she actually did?"

"Ugh...no. B-but I'm pretty sure it came from her direction!"

Pretty sure, huh? Not enough to go on. Did Noela smack her accidentally?

"Noela not slap! Swear!"

"Don't worry, Noela. I know you'd never do that."

"Master...Master really is Noela's master. Love!"

Just as she was about to embrace me—*zaaaap!* I felt a mysterious stabbing pain in my hand.

"Gah! Ow!" *What just happened?!*

"What wrong, Master?!"

"Er, Noela, did you just..."

"You're grown up, Mr. Reiji," Vivi said. "You shouldn't make weird noises like that."

"Pipe down. Even grown-ups yell sometimes." *Seriously, what the hell* was *that? It definitely came from Noela.* "So that's what you were talking about, Vivi."

STOPPING THE SHOCKS

"Now you understand?!"

"Wait. Could that have been...?" I inched away from Noela. So did Vivi.

Noela tilted her head as we circled her. "Garoo? What wrong?"

"You used a superpower to punch us in the blink of an eye! Right, Mr. Reiji?!"

"Hold up, Vivi. If that were true, Noela would totally be on the hook for acting mean on purpose. But this little fluffball's got no clue what she did!"

An unintentional attack so fast, Vivi and I couldn't see it... Wait, we're having dry weather, aren't we? "Ah! I know!" I exclaimed. "Static electricity!"

"She attacked us with static electricity?" Vivi asked, then nodded solemnly. Apparently, she'd at least heard of it.

"Stat tick electricity? What that, Master?"

"You know how sometimes, when you grab a doorknob, it zaps you?"

"Noela know! Always happen!"

"That's a static shock," I explained. During the winter, static would zap you all over when you undressed; it was maddening. In short, Noela had shocked Vivi—and me—with static electricity. "Noela's incredibly fluffy. She probably conducts electricity easily."

"Noela no want static attack, Master."

"I know. Hang on a few minutes."

My medicine-making skill was reacting; it seemed I could formulate something to deal with static. I left the store in Vivi's hands. Once I'd chosen the ingredients I needed in the lab, Noela entered. "Noela help!"

"O-okay."

Having gotten shocked already, I couldn't drop my guard. That said, it would probably be fine if Noela pitched in, since she'd already discharged quite a bit of static. We got to work; the new product took about two hours to finish.

SHOCKPROOF LIQUID: Apply a few drops to prevent static shock.

Heck yeah! No more getting zapped.

"Let's see how it works on the fluffy one," I said to myself, sprinkling some shockproof liquid on Noela right away. I know the frequent shocks were aggravating her, since they happened at random, and they were certainly bugging Vivi and me.

"No more zapping?"

"You should be a-okay now."

She trotted over and leapt onto my back. "Noela no zap you!"

"Thank goodness!"

I'm sure plenty of folks deal with static during the winter, I reflected. *I should probably make more shockproof liquid for the store.*

Later, I sprinkled Vivi with the liquid as well, ending the random shocks.

◆◆◆

A few days later, Doz—the Red Cat Brigade's vice captain—stared at a bottle of shockproof liquid intently.

"You having static electricity issues, Doz?" I asked.

"Well, yeah, but they ain't major," he replied. "Still, this shockproof stuff looks amazing, Medicine God!"

"Not at all! It just protects you from static."

"A guy in our squad uses electric magic," Doz continued. "It's not crazy strong or anything, but…well, I just wonder what'd happen if I sprinkled this on myself, and he hit me with some magic. Imagine if this anti-static stuff protected me!"

"I doubt it would. I didn't design it with attack magic in mind."

"But if it did, that'd be crazy!"

"It certainly would be," I agreed. "I don't know how I'd feel about testing that on a human, though."

Doz looked incredibly determined. "Gimme a bottle," he ordered.

H-he's down to try it?

And so, Doz bought the shockproof liquid and headed home, not to be seen for some time. The failed experiment had probably resulted in a charred Doz—or so I thought.

One day, the drugstore had a rather rare customer: a tough-looking old man wearing a suit of armor. "I am Zain, captain of the Granad Knights. I came upon hearing of your shop's shockproof liquid."

I stood there blankly for a second, taken aback by his powerful presence. "Oh, um, er…yes, we have some."

"I've heard this product of yours grants resistance to lightning magic."

"Wait. Who'd you hear that from?" *S-seriously?! Doz's little experiment worked?*

"Your shockproof liquid is already famous in my profession, good sir!" Zain declared.

For real?

"Well, I designed it for…" I explained the product's original purpose to Zain.

"Hmm. I see. You created it to protect you from static electricity?"

"Yes. I couldn't stand it if someone got hurt using it for something else."

STOPPING THE SHOCKS

"Gah ha ha ha! Fear not, young man. That'd be better than us heading into battle with no plan and getting attacked!"

Attacked? Before I could tilt my head in confusion, Zain requested five hundred bottles of shockproof liquid immediately. I explained that the order would take about a month, since I also made other products, and he signed off on it.

◆●◆

Four weeks later, I passed the crates of shockproof liquid to one of Zain's knights. The next day, Ejil came to work grimacing.

"Listen to this, Doctor! Those dastardly humans have gotten smarter!"

Has he completely forgotten that I'm human?

"Electric magic doesn't work on them anymore!" Ejil continued. "This proves I can never underestimate knowledgeable beings with technical expertise!"

Whoops. Er, my bad, Ejil.

DRUGSTORE in another world
~ The Slow Life of a Cheat Pharmacist ~

The Softness Contest

20

"**I**T'S ALMOST TIME to switch out this towel," Mina noted as she began folding the laundry.

She placed the towel to one side, then continued folding the rest. As she reached for my underwear, she wavered. Looking bashful, she folded them with the skill you'd expect of someone used to the task.

Now that I think about it, Mina does *wash and fold my underwear. Man, I'm sure slow only to notice that now.*

"M-Mom?"

"Hmm? What's that, Mr. Reiji?"

"Er...nothing." I fell silent, sensing Mina's rage in my future. Then I looked at the towel she'd put aside, which often hung by the sink; it had gotten old, ragged, and rough. "Hmm. I never actually got around to making that, did I?"

"Is something wrong?" Mina asked.

"Nope. I just realized that I never made the stuff that goes with laundry detergent."

"What stuff?" She tilted her head.

Of course, Mina was puzzled. I had yet to hear about anyone in Kalta using fabric softener, and I'd certainly never seen it in this world.

Mina was now folding Noela's underwear. "What exactly are you staring at, Mr. Reiji?" She shot me a narrow-eyed glare.

"Er, nothing!" I looked away, panicking.

I *was* a little curious about the beastling's—er, werewolf's—underwear; I mean, I'd always wondered what was going on with her tail. Furthermore, Noela used to be anxious to show me her underclothes.

"Look, Master!"

"Hell no."

"Panties make men happy!"

"Who the heck taught you that?"

"Noela's panties make Master happy?!"

"Definitely not."

"Groo..."

I recalled her looking particularly downtrodden at that point. *Where'd she pick that "panties make men happy" thing up? Man, if she does that again, we'll have to talk. Anyway, I should make this stuff before I forget.*

THE SOFTNESS CONTEST

Frankly, I had no idea whether this world even needed fabric softener. It might've been unnecessary, or impossible to make. I had no clue. *But hey, once I create some, I'll see how the girls react.*

I headed to the lab and got cracking. Fortunately, I didn't need special ingredients; I could formulate the product just by mixing the right quantities of things I had.

> **ROSE-SCENTED FABRIC SOFTENER:** Makes fabric soft and fluffy. Smells like roses.

Perfect. "Mina?"

"Yes?"

I called her into the lab. "Could you do me a big favor and pour this into your next load of laundry, along with the detergent?"

"What is it?"

"Heh heh! You'll see."

"It's not anything weird, right?"

"I promise it's not. Don't worry. Oh—could you put this in too?" I handed her the old towel she'd put aside.

"If you like. But I was actually thinking of throwing that towel away." Since I hadn't explained the fabric softener's use, Mina was appropriately confused. I passed her the bottle; she raised her eyebrows. "Ooh! This smells lovely."

"It's rose-scented."

"I understand! Your new product makes laundry smell like roses!" Mina thought she'd solved the riddle.

"That's not all!"

"I-I'm so curious! I can't wait to try it!"

I'd seemingly piqued Mina's domestic curiosity. She headed off, and I followed closely behind. Filling the laundry tub with water, she added the rough towel, some detergent, and the fabric softener.

"And now I just wash them as usual?" she asked.

"Exactly."

Mina scrubbed away; the scent of roses drifted from the tub. "The aroma is lovely! It'll be nice to smell flowers while I wash clothes."

That's not all, sweetheart!

After scrubbing the towel, she set it out to dry. "Um…besides the rose scent, I haven't noticed anything different."

"The towel has to dry first."

"Really?" Mina again tilted her head.

The towel dried off quickly, since it was nice and bright out. Three hours later, I said, "Mina, it's about time."

"Okay. I'll get that towel." She put on her slippers, then headed to the clothesline and grabbed it. "Huh?! Wh-what the…? It feels so…" She pressed the towel against

THE SOFTNESS CONTEST

her cheek. "It used to be really scratchy. Now it's so soft, and it smells great!"

"Right?"

"This is incredible, Mr. Reiji! I want to use that new product on all of our fabric right away!" Mina rubbed the towel against her face with an ecstatic expression. "I can't ever go back to doing laundry without it!"

I took the towel. "Whoa! This must be setting a new world record for softness. I've created a doggone gosh-darn monster fabric softener!" The towel was so jaw-droppingly pillowy that I blurted out nonsense. *I lived alone on Earth, so I didn't use fabric softener much. This stuff is crazy!*

"We might not need Noela anymore," Mina joked as we passed the towel back and forth.

"This towel's even fluffier than her," I agreed.

Noela was watching us through the window. "No! That no good, Master!"

Apparently sensing that the towel was outshining her, she rushed up wagging her tail. "Master! Noela's tail! Touch as much as want!"

"I'm good," I replied. "I'm focused on this amazing artificial softness right now."

"Garoo!" Noela wailed. Looking around and spotting the bottle of fabric softener, she picked it up and sniffed it. "Groo?! Smell...good!"

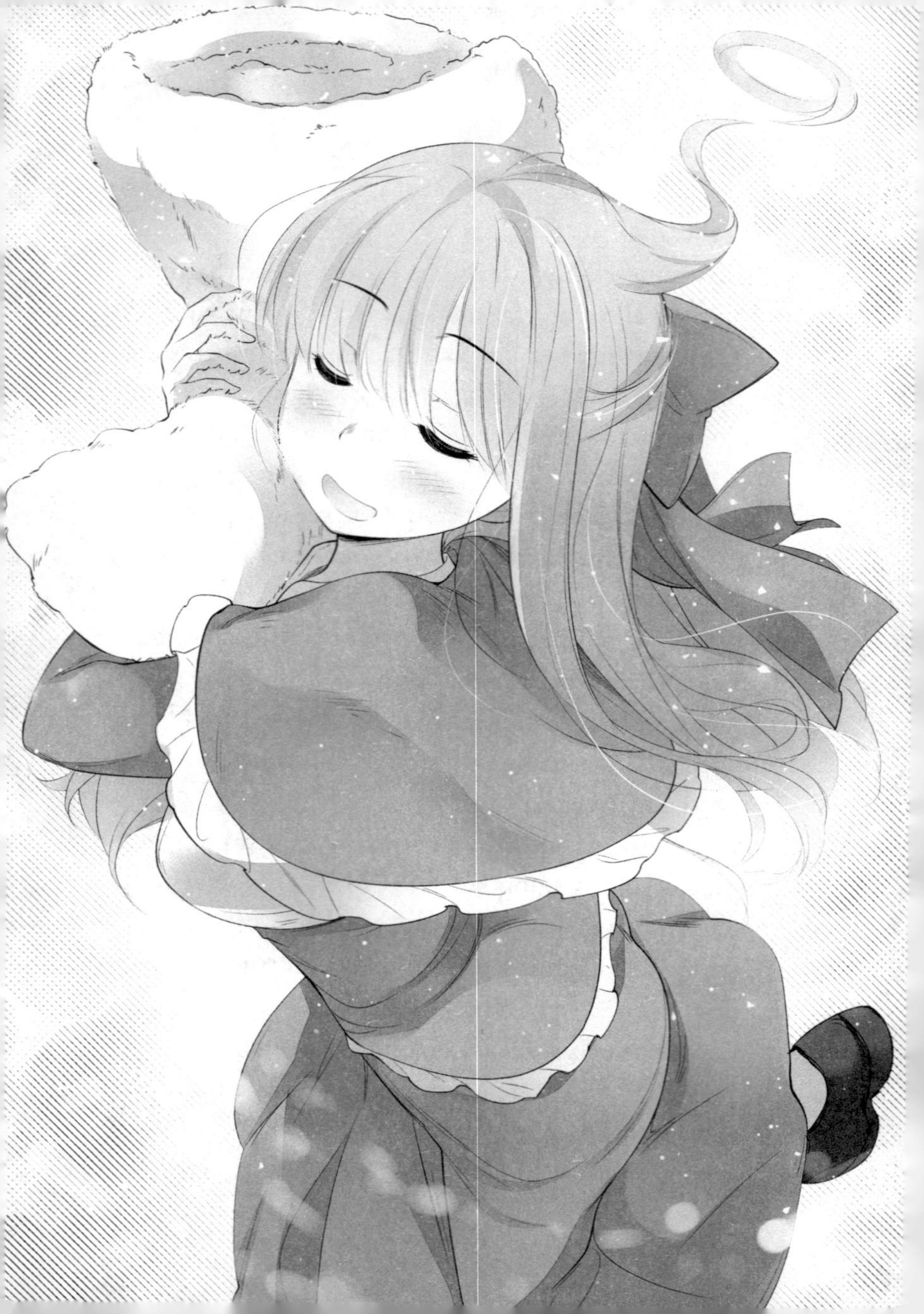

THE SOFTNESS CONTEST

"Right?" *I guess the fluffy one finally gets it.*

Noela popped the cap off the bottle.

"Hey! that's not drinkable."

"Arroo?!" yelped Noela, so astonished that her fur stood on end. She gaped at me, not understanding how I'd known she would try sipping the fabric softener.

I offered Noela the towel, but she swatted it away with her tail. She was set on viewing it as her rival and refused to experience its softness firsthand.

"Let's stock this new product at the drugstore, Mr. Reiji!" Mina urged. "I'm sure it'll sell well."

"Hold your horses, Mina. As far as we're concerned, this towel's awesomely soft—but other people might not be impressed."

"I'm really not sure that's the case," she insisted.

I get what she's saying, but how humiliating would it be if the fabric softener didn't sell? If we could demonstrate its effects in public somehow, that'd be awesome. "What if we took this stuff to the Red Cat Brigade?"

"Oh! That's a great idea," said Mina, as she began washing our sheets.

"No! No wash Noela's!" The fluffy werewolf continued to object.

I carried the leftover fabric softener to the Red Cat Brigade's quarters in the center of town.

"Hey, guys! It's Reiji from Kirio Drugs!" I heard busy footsteps beyond the door.

Annabelle appeared. "What—it's just you? It's rare that you show your face 'round here."

The off-duty mercenaries inside watched through the windows and front door, grinning for some reason.

Annabelle's fingers twirled her red ponytail. "W-wanna come in?" She looked away. "Would you like some tea?"

"Actually, I'm here with a request," I said, handing her the fabric softener. "It'd be awesome if you could try this stuff out."

"What's this?" she asked. "Whoa! It smells great."

A Red Cat Brigade member poked his head through the window and offered his theory. "I'm sure it's special perfume he made just for you, Boss! He must've come here to give it to y—gurmph!"

Annabelle hurled her slipper directly into his face, her cheeks bright red. "A-as if! You're a bunch of dumb kids, I swear." She glared at her men like a street punk keeping a stiff upper lip.

I guess he was right that this is *kind of a present, though,* I reflected, then gave Annabelle the lowdown on how to use the fabric softener.

"Hunh. You put it in the laundry, eh? And it'll make our clothes all soft and nice-smellin'?"

THE SOFTNESS CONTEST

"Yup. Give it a shot."

"Figured it was somethin' like that," she replied.

The mercs whispered among themselves.

"The boss is disappointed."

"'Cause you got her hopes up! You said it was a present!"

"Shut up! That's what it looked like!"

Annabelle shook with rage. "Shut the hell up, and get your asses back inside!"

"Sorry, Boss!" The men retreated quickly into the building.

"Ahem!" She cleared her throat. "Anyhow, sure. I'll try it for you."

"Much obliged."

◆●◆

A few days later, Annabelle swung by the drugstore.

"Oh, hey!" I greeted her. "How was that fabric softener?"

"How was it? Crazy! I can't believe how soft and nice-smellin' everythin' is now! Clothes, towels, you name it!"

"Glad to hear it."

"Also, uh...you know how my men are all kinda mama's boys?" she added. "I guess those soft, rose-scented clothes remind 'em of their moms back home. Five guys in a row have requested time off!"

"Ah. I totally get that."

"It's a real problem," Annabelle griped, smiling.

Looks like this fabric softener will sell, I concluded. *We'll start carrying it at the drugstore.*

"Red girl!" called Noela, who was watching the store with me.

"Hm? What's up, wolf girl?"

"Which better? Noela's tail, or soft towel?"

Noela's still holding a grudge?

"Uh...I'd say your tail."

"Garroo! Red gets it!" The werewolf shot a victorious gaze my way. "Touch Noela's tail, Master! Noela best!"

And so, Noela got her groove back.

21

The Clean-Shaven King

ONE DAY AT SUNSET, I saw Ririka the elf wandering around outside the drugstore.

What's she doing? If she's buying something, she should just come in. "Hey, Ririka."

"Eek!"

"Mina isn't here. She's shopping."

"I'm not here to see Mina."

"Oh. I figured you were looking for her."

"That's not why I came by." Ririka cleared her throat, trying to change the subject. "It's kind of hard to explain why I'm here. Um…I need to confide in you."

"You sure? In *me*?"

Now and then, female customers consulted Mina about issues they didn't want to explain to me. There were lots of sensitive things women preferred not to discuss with men; at least, that's what Mina told me once.

Ririka thought it over for a moment and nodded. "Um...I heard the drugstore has a treatment that...gets rid of hair."

"Hair-removal cream? Yeah, we do."

"That's not what I mean. Um...ugh! Why do *I* have to buy this?!" Cradling her head in embarrassment, Ririka continued, "Hair-removal cream isn't powerful enough. I'm asking for something stronger."

"Seriously?" Our hair-removal cream was designed to get rid of pesky hairs easily.

"You're a man, Reiji—wh-what do you use?" Ririka asked hesitantly.

"What do you mean?"

"Well, um, you get stubble, right?"

"Oh. Not much. I'm good from shaving every three days."

When I'd first arrived in Kalta, I wasn't used to this world's razors; I'd nicked myself repeatedly. Now, though, shaving was no big deal. Still, why was Ririka asking about that? "Wait, don't tell me...!"

"I-It's not what you think!" Ririka shrieked. "I'm not growing a beard!"

No? For real?

THE CLEAN-SHAVEN KING

"Don't look so doubtful!"

"My bad. But if you're talking about hair as tough as facial stubble..." *And if she needs something that works like hair-removal cream...* "Uh, o-okay, wait here! I'm g-gonna go get Mina."

"Why're you freaking out?"

"I mean, do you want to talk to *me* about such a delicate spot?"

"You've got it all wrong, you dummy!" Ririka shrieked. She blushed; steam nearly came out her ears. "It's for Kururu's beard!"

"Oh, so *that's* it! You should've said so earlier! I was freaking out."

"No, *I* was!"

Since there were no other customers, I had Ririka sit so we could talk properly. "Kururu's beard has gotten really thick recently, and he can't shave it very well," she explained. "He tried your hair-removal cream, but it didn't last long, and his beard got even thicker."

"For real? That cream suppresses hair growth." *Is he absurdly hairy or something?* "Why isn't Kururu here to consult me himself?"

"He said, 'I could never face Reiji baby like this!' He got furious at me for suggesting it."

"What is he, a child?!"

"He's just weirdly modest sometimes."

Ririka had it tough. I understood why she'd had such a hard time explaining the issue.

"However much he shaves, he gets five o'clock shadow," she sighed. "I came here hoping you could help."

"Uh-huh. I get it now," I assured her. "I've never had that issue with my stubble, so I've never formulated anything for it."

Kalta's citizens didn't seem to care about shaving their facial hair. The old farmers, innkeeper, and general store owner all had beards. Actually, it was much rarer to see someone *without* some sort of beard or mustache. *In Japan, you typically shave before work,* I reflected. *But hey, it makes sense that my culture is different.*

Still, I supposed there were exceptions to the rule in this world, like Ririka's delicate brother.

"Do you think you can make something more powerful?" she asked.

"Yup. After all, we had stronger hair-removal products in the other world."

"Other world?" she tilted her head.

"Never mind," I said quickly, then asked her to wait a bit.

I was the only one home, but since the drugstore had had few walk-ins today, I figured it'd be okay to leave for a couple minutes. I entered the lab and started working.

THE CLEAN-SHAVEN KING

So that occasionally cleft-chinned Kururu's got five o'clock shadow, huh? Man, his character just keeps evolving.

Since Kalta didn't have the same facial-hair styles as Japan, I wasn't sure whether I could sell the product I was creating. Still, there was no harm in making some.

"This should work just fine."

> **CLEAN-SHAVEN KING SHAVING GEL:** Provides smooth shaving experience when used on thick hair. Creates protective layer between skin and razor, moisturizing and preventing cuts.

Mina got home just as I finished. When I headed back into the drugstore, she and Ririka were chatting. "Perfect timing, Mina! Can you watch the store?"

"I'm happy to. Are you going out?"

"Uh...well, yeah. Not that I want to. I'm heading to Kururu's."

"Oh, all right! Take care!"

Ririka and I left together. I showed her the shaving gel.

"Is this really a new product? You didn't take long to make it."

"It wasn't very complicated," I replied. "I've made something similar before."

"I see." Ririka seemed content with that.

I followed her quite a distance from town to the elven woods. I'd heard about the area before, but this was my first time visiting. The forest was clearly well cultivated, unlike the others I'd been to.

We passed lots of elves as we went farther in; I hadn't seen many of them in town. It all felt new to me—especially because, up till now, the only elves I'd gotten to know were Kururu and Ririka.

Finally, we arrived at the house where the siblings lived together.

"Here we are." Ririka opened the door and peeked inside. "Brother? Reiji made you a new treatment."

"Really?! Reiji baby did that for me?"

Ririka gestured for me to enter, so I followed her in. "Hey."

"Eek!" Kururu let out a rather feminine shriek, seeking cover. "Wh-what're you doing here?!"

"Well, I haven't actually tested this stuff yet," I replied. "I want to see its effects in person."

"I'm delighted that you're worried about your crush's plight, but since I'm dealing with a personal emergency—"

His stubble is a personal emergency? Not even knowing when to interrupt, I opted to ignore his complaints entirely. "Hold Kururu down, Ririka."

"All right!"

THE CLEAN-SHAVEN KING

"Wh-what're you doing?! Stop that, Ririka! I-I can't possibly show Reiji my stubble!"

"Oh, shut up for once!" Ririka smacked him.

Kururu toppled over with a loud thud. *Will he be okay?*

"I think Kururu will keep quiet for a bit, Reiji!" Ririka exclaimed. "Now's your chance!"

"Uh...what do you mean? I'm pretty sure you knocked him out."

Ririka rolled her prone brother onto his back.

I gasped. "Talk about five o'clock shadow! That's unbelievably fast hair growth."

"He looks fine after he shaves, but then it grows right in."

That stubble's ridiculous—is it trying to match his personality?

Ririka handed me a shaving brush, and I plastered some drugstore gel around Kururu's mouth. Then I had her bring her brother's razor. "You should really leave this sort of thing to the pros, but..."

"It's fine. Do what you have to."

"Could you get me some gloves? I don't want to risk ending up super hairy."

"Wha—?! Is stubble contagious?!"

Not at all, but I don't want it sticking to my bare hands!

Pulling on the gloves, I gripped the razor and started shaving. *Swish...swoosh...swish...*

"Whoa—amazing! Bare skin! My brother finally looks like himself!"

"This is actually pretty fun," I said.

Ririka was nearly weeping. *This really makes her that happy?*

"Thank goodness, Kururu," she murmured. "Now you won't have to shave every half hour."

"You weren't kidding when you said this was a problem, huh?"

"He can finally depart this world clean-shaven."

"He ain't dead!"

We kept babbling for about ten minutes, and the old Kururu finally emerged. I'd been nervous, because I'd never shaved someone else; thanks to the gel, though, I managed not to cut him. As the finishing touch, I spread some hair-removal cream on Kururu's face, since it slowed hair growth.

"Wake up, brother!"

"Don't. He'll just be a pain."

We'd gotten rid of the thick-haired elf's five o'clock shadow.

◆◆◆

THE CLEAN-SHAVEN KING

A few days later, I put the shaving gel on sale. Once I described it to the drugstore's male customers, it proved a decent seller. At the end of the day, I guess everyone wants a comfortable shave.

DRUGSTORE in another world
~ The Slow Life of a Cheat Pharmacist ~

Afterword

Howdy, everyone! It's me, Kennoji.

Thanks to all your support, I released a third volume of *Drugstore in Another World!* I'm grateful.

The manga adaptation on Web Comic Gamma Plus is doing well! Oh, and Volume One of the manga came out alongside Volume Three of the light novel. The way Eri Haruno-sensei draws Noela is just adorable. I advise everyone to check out the manga to see how cute she is!

My other title, *Hazure Skill: The Guild Member with a Worthless Skill Is Actually a Legendary Assassin*, is currently available in stores. The manga adaptation is also being published among ComicWalker's isekai titles. Please take a look if you're interested!

That's it for self-promotion! Now I'd like to say thanks to everyone who helped me reach this point.

To my editors: thank you for not only considering my opinions, but also skillfully putting together the lovely cover design. I plan to give my all to Brave Bunko going forward, so thanks again for your support!

To Matsuuni-sensei: thanks for all this volume's top-quality illustrations. The characters are meant to be comforting presences, and every time I receive new art from you, I feel wonderful.

I'd also like to thank everyone who had anything to do with publishing this series.

Finally, thank you, dear reader. Those of you in the bookstore, reading the afterword early: feel free to take this book to the register!

I'm going to keep putting my all into this. I hope you stay with me!

—Kennoji

FROM THE AUTHOR
Kennoji

I was making a point of going running four or five times a week, but during the winter, I skipped a bunch of jogs and gained a lot of weight...a whole lot of weight (too bad). Please, someone, make me some weight-loss medicine!

Let your imagination take flight with Seven Seas' light novel imprint: Airship

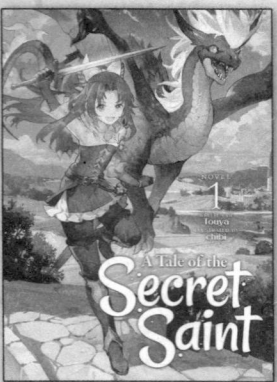

- A Tale of the Secret Saint
- She Professed Herself Pupil of the Wise Man
- Monster Musume: Monster Girls on the Job!
- The Haunted Bookstore - Gateway to a Parallel Universe
- Loner Life in Another World
- I Swear I Won't Bother You Again!

Discover your next great read at
www.airshipnovels.com